My Ea...

Audrey Harrison
Published by Audrey Harrison
© Copyright 2016 Audrey Harrison
Audrey Harrison asserts the moral right to be identified as the author of this work.

This novel is entirely a work of fiction. The names, characters and incidents portrayed in it are the work of the author's imagination. Any resemblance to actual persons, living or dead, events or localities is entirely coincidental.

This eBook is licensed for your personal enjoyment only. This eBook may not be re-sold or given away to other people.

Thank you for respecting the hard work of this author.

Find more about the author and contact details at the end of this book.

*

This book was proof read by Joan Kelley. Read more about Joan at the end of this story, but if you need her, you may reach her at oh1kelley@gmail.com.

Prologue

Dorset 1806

Henry, Earl of Grinstead leaned against the wall. He must be getting old; the operation had nearly come unstuck. If the raid had gone wrong, the lives of his men could have been lost. A year ago that thought would not have affected him, but tonight–tonight he went cold at the different scenarios that could have happened. It was more good luck than good judgement that had saved the day. He let out a long breath; not for the first time, the thought flickered into his mind that he wanted a change.

Millicent Holland, cousin of Baron Glazebrook and chaperone of Miss Baker, respectively, stormed around the edge of the building where Henry had sought a moment's refuge from the scene of arrests and uproar that was currently taking place on the estate of Baron Glazebrook.

Milly came to a halt before Henry and put her hands on her hips. She blazed with anger; Henry would wonder later if he had actually seen flames flaring at him from her eyes.

"You nearly got them killed!" Milly hissed at Henry. Those who knew her would be astounded if they heard Milly's tone, or the fact that she was berating the great Lord Grinstead. His position in society, handsome features and confident air would have been enough to silence most people if disagreeing with him. But Milly was not afraid of the man standing before her; oh, he was older than she and had far more influence and power; even more than she had guessed, if the evening's events were anything to go by, but it did not matter; his actions had threatened her family.

"But I didn't," Henry responded, easily falling back into his normal devil-may-care slightly cold attitude.

"That was because of Charles's actions to save his sister; you didn't give a fig about what could have happened to them!"

"So, the young Baron is a hero in everyone's eyes and can live on his brave deed for the rest of his days. I'm surprised he's not shaking my hand in thanks," came the derisive response.

Henry must have been more bone tired than he thought because he did not see the slap coming. His head whipped to the side with the force of Milly's hand striking him across the face. She might be slightly built, but a strike fuelled by anger hit its mark well.

"Don't you dare speak so carelessly about my cousins!" Milly hissed. She had never hated anyone in her life; in fact, she took pride in the knowledge that she could face most things with calmness. Tonight's events had stretched her to the limit, and only one person was responsible for it in her eyes.

Henry tenderly touched the outside of his cheek; he could taste blood on his tongue. "Most people would be dead after delivering a blow like that," he said quietly.

"That doesn't surprise me! You're obviously easy with anyone's life except your own. Let's just say that it's a warning from me to you to stay away from my family," Milly ground out. She had the overwhelming urge to continue slapping him until she saw something other than coldness in his hazel eyes.

"Anyone who mixes with smugglers and thieves will always be fair game, Miss Holland." Henry had to admire the spinster, despite wishing her a million miles away; not many would stand up to him the way she was doing.

"It just proves what sort of a man you are if you go about risking lives so carelessly. Looking after the country's safety includes considering all the people who live here not just the higher members of society!"

Henry paused for a moment; she was right. He had become so focused on Joshua Shambles that he had forgotten what was at risk; people could have died, and Joshua had escaped capture anyway. What was worse, the scoundrel now knew that Henry was on his trail. He looked at Milly standing before him, glaring at him with the same disgust and contempt that had started to creep into his own expressions when gazing at his reflection. He had started to avoid mirrors to try and block out the feelings that he needed to keep constrained if he was to be effective.

Henry gritted his teeth; he was being a sentimental fool; of course, lives would be put at risk. They were at war with a man who, for the greater part, seemed unstoppable; who the hell did she think she was questioning him? "You have no idea what you are talking about. Go back to your drawing books, Miss Holland and leave the professionals to keep you safe." His tone was bored and dismissive.

Milly sneered at Henry. "If my safety is dependent on the likes of you, thank goodness I can handle myself. I dread to think what would happen if you were faced with real criminals; you couldn't even arrest a bunch of smugglers without their ringleader escaping!"

Milly had hit Henry's pride, shame and guilty conscience in two sentences, and he reacted badly. He took hold of Milly by the tops of her arms and dragged her closer to him. Lowering his face so that their faces were inches apart, gritting his teeth, he almost spat the words out. "You protect yourself? Ha! That's a joke indeed! You while the hours away drawing or playing some inane instrument while, yes, I do try and protect the likes of you! From the look of you, you've never seen an angry man in your life! Tell me this: what would you do if faced by the men your family has seen tonight? Would you stab them with a pencil? What about the man that had his throat slit so badly that he could no longer speak but could still fight off half a dozen excise men? I'd bring him to you only he blew himself apart rather than face capture. I would have loved to see you stand up to him. These men are not the fops that frequented the ballrooms when you were in your youth; don't confuse the two."

Henry did not wait for a response from Milly. Some madness had stirred him, and he pressed his mouth roughly against hers, and he kissed her like no gentleman should ever kiss a genteel lady. He possessed her, dragging her into an embrace, pulling her roughly against his hard body.

Milly was tall but slightly built. It felt as if she had been enveloped by a strong beast, but with such passion that it literally took her breath away. She had been kissed before, but not in the manner she was being kissed now. Instead of pushing him away, she used her hands to grab his hair and keep his head bent to hers. The growl the movement caused sent the nerve ends through her body jumping to life.

All too soon, Henry pushed Milly away, not as roughly as he had grabbed her, but the movement forced her to step away from him; he still held her arms loosely, making her wonder if she was going to be pulled towards him again. "You can't even fight off the advances of the likes of me! What use would you be against someone really intent on doing you serious harm?" he asked with derision.

Milly stiffened at Henry's words. His words stung more than he could ever have hoped. Milly cursed her weakness as her eyes pooled with tears; she never cried; she had trained herself not to feel so much, but somehow his rejection reminded her of another time when she had not been good enough and, for some reason, it seemed to hurt even more this time, which was ridiculous.

Milly looked at Henry. Her eyes might betray her inner feelings, but she met his glare fully. "I think you have said quite enough, Lord Grinstead. I would be grateful if you could release me; I shall return to the house; I have, after all, drawings and such inane occupations that require my urgent attention."

Henry released her without a word and stood leaning against the wall once more. He watched the young woman carefully. He had offended her; he had intended to do it, showing a side of him that he would never have shown in any respectable drawing room; only those who were closest to him knew of the block of ice that lived where his heart should have been. She had reacted violently once, but in reality he knew she would not react again; when making a hit, Henry always made sure he hit the target. She had not known what she had unleashed.

Milly straightened her spencer and pulled her skirt straight. Her movements were graceful. "Good evening, Lord Grinstead. I hope our paths never cross again." She walked away from him with her head held high. He would not see the tears that would be shed during the night hours. She would never acknowledge openly how much he had hurt her.

Henry ran his hands through his hair in frustration. He should follow her and beg her forgiveness; he had been a first class devil, and she had not deserved to be treated in such a way. She had reacted angrily because her family had been in danger; it was understandable; it was commendable.

He turned and leaned his arm against the wall, resting his head on his sleeve, breathing deeply when he thought of the tears his words and actions had caused. He never felt remorse, but there had been dignity in the way she had responded; if he had a heart it would have been affected. Again, he blew out a breath; she was better off without any more antagonism from him; he would not inflict further damage to her that contact with him would undoubtedly bring.

He stood upright; he had a job to complete, and he was going to do it. His pride depended on him carrying out the promise he had vowed to himself. No one could get in the way and, if her kisses were anything to go by, she could quite easily get in the way. No, Miss Millicent Holland was better off as far away from the Earl of Grinstead as she could possibly be.

Unfortunately for Miss Holland and the Earl of Grinstead, fate had other plans.

Chapter 1

Two weeks later.

The wedding of Miss Clara Baker and Edmund Ainscough, the Earl of Chertsey was always going to be a small affair. Edmund was not prepared to put his bride in any more danger than she had faced already because of his interference in her life. Admittedly, if he had not interfered he would not be standing in front of a clergyman, marrying the only woman that he had ever cared anything for.

He had forgiven his friend, Henry Howarth for his hand in the fiasco that still haunted Edmund's dreams. In reality, Henry was the only person he would have standing at his side as witness to the proceedings. Apart from Clara's brother Charles and Milly, the cousin to the family and previously Clara's companion, the church was empty.

Edmund was marrying his bride and then taking her far away from the Somerset coast to enjoy a long holiday in Scotland. He wanted to be at the other end of the country from Mr John Beckett at the Home Office, who along with Henry had persuaded him to join the Secret Service. Mr Beckett had decided that he wanted to employ some of the higher echelons of society to try and gather information from every level; usually a spy was from the lower ranks. Edmund had been persuaded as one who stood a little on the outside of society, and the thought appealed to his more nonconformist side. Now, though, he wanted to be the furthest distance as he could from the Home Office, the South coast and anyone else who knew them for as long as possible.

Clara looked beautiful in her ivory satin pelisse, which had tiny pearl buttons running from its collar all the way to the floor. He would enjoy undoing every one of those buttons very late that night when they were hours away from their present location. He had nearly lost her on the night when the smuggling ring had tried to land Frenchmen and explosives on her brother's land in an effort to launch an attack on the King. She had survived, and he was damn well sure he was not going to risk her again while some of the gang of criminals were still at large.

Milly stood just behind the bride, watching her darling Clara marry the man she loved. Milly had been suspicious of Edmund's motives at first, but it was clear to everyone that he adored his new wife, and she was happy her cousin had found a man who they now realised thought so highly of her. Milly would have enjoyed the service far more if Henry was not also in attendance. They had not seen one another since that horrible night. Milly was still affected by everything that had happened; it was not easy to forget that the smugglers were prepared to leave Charles and Clara to drown but, in some respects, her run-in with Henry haunted her more.

It grated on her nerves that he seemed so calm, so sure of himself, and she still flushed when she remembered what had gone on between them. They had both lashed out, but Henry more effectively than Milly. What he had said to her had sliced right through her heart. His words rang in her ears, reminding her of another conversation so long ago.

She stood tall and faced the front. That time was dead and buried now, there no was point going over the past; she had been looking to the future for these last four years; she had to keep doing that. What was done was done.

Henry might have looked relaxed and calm, but he had watched Milly as a hawk watched its prey since she had walked into the church. She was dignified; he acknowledged that; she had gracefully followed her cousins down the aisle, looking elegant in her deep blue pelisse. Her hair framed her face, dark curls peeping out of the sides of her bonnet. He wondered idly if she realised how closely he was watching her; she was refusing to look in his direction, her clear grey eyes focused only on what was going on with the happy couple, which made his lips twitch in amusement. He was not usually so completely ignored and it amused him.

Henry pondered to himself about those pivotal events at Glazebrook House; it was normal to go over time and again an incident after it had come to a head, especially when one of the wanted men had managed to escape. The problem Henry had with it all was that it was the end of that night that haunted the dark hours when he could not sleep. It was her kisses that had him tossing and turning and the look in her eyes when he had made his verbal hit that had him staring at the canopy of his four-poster bed.

He cursed himself to hell and back. Seeing her today would only increase his turmoil. It did tickle him that she refused to look in his direction, but the slight flush on her cheeks betrayed her aloof exterior; no, Miss Holland, you are not as unmoved as you act, Henry thought with some modicum of pleasure.

She was quietly intelligent; he had seen that when the group was acting under the pretence of friendship; Henry's need to watch the crook, Joshua Shambles, who had befriended the young Baron, Charles Baker, had suddenly made the whole family interesting to Henry and Edmund. Henry had wondered why the pretty, intelligent Miss Holland was unmarried, because she *was* pretty, having the same dark hair as her cousin, Clara, but Milly's clear grey eyes were unusual in comparison to her cousin's blue.

Those grey eyes seemed to miss little as she had been chaperone, cousin and friend to her relations. A protector that had reacted like a mother protecting her young. A shame she was on the shelf and would never experience motherhood, Henry thought to himself before raising his eyes to heaven and letting out a breath. He must be going addled if he was mourning for the unborn children of a spinster! He really needed to get hold of himself.

After the service the party returned to the London home of Clara's brother Charles, on Half Moon Street, for the wedding breakfast. Henry was seated opposite Milly, which further amused him as he could tell she wished him to Jericho but, although he watched her, he concentrated on entertaining Charles who was bemoaning the fact that he had to wait another month until he married his darling Miss Beresford.

"Let Miss Beresford have the pleasure of planning every stage of her grand affair," Clara responded teasingly. Brother and sister were back on easy terms, something that had not been the case over the previous few months because of his friendship with Joshua Shambles.

"You didn't want a grand affair!" Charles grumbled. "I'd have been happy with a celebration like yours."

"Yes, but you are sociable and will enjoy the fuss and attention; my husband would hate it," Clara responded, smiling at her new husband.

Edmund smiled lovingly at his wife, all traces of the arrogantly bored Earl that once existed disappeared. "I would've done it for you, but it still had to happen as soon as possible." He refused to wait for any length of time before they could be together legitimately; he had barely left her side since that night in Dorset, not wanting to rely on anyone else with her care and protection.

"It would've been impossible to arrange!" Clara laughed, knowing full well that her husband would have hated a large wedding. After the previous few weeks she had not wished to have too many people at the venue; she felt uneasy that Joshua Shambles was at large, mainly for the safety of her brother, but she was aware that he now must hate them all with a vengeance. The thought of which was a niggle that would not go away.

"I wasn't prepared to wait. I don't trust anyone else to look after you as well as I can," Edmund responded with a shrug. He was determined never to let his wife out of his sight if he could help it. The thought that he could have lost her still shook him to his core.

"I can look after myself, thank you!" Clara said primly.

"I'm happy to watch from close by then," Edmund said softly, kissing his wife's hand.

A silence descended on the small group, each one slightly envious of such open adoration on the part of the happy couple.

Clara smiled at her husband before turning to her cousin. "When we return I want you to come and live with us," she said.

Milly flushed slightly at the thought that Henry was party to this particular conversation. "Clara, we've discussed this already," she said patiently, but firmly.

"I'm to stay with Charles until he's married, keeping house for him, and then I'm to return home."

"But-," Clara started, wanting to raise the same objections she had every time Milly mentioned returning to her home. The cousins were partly aware of what that would involve, although Milly had never fully confided in her cousins, but they knew enough to be concerned for her. Clara wanted to protect her beloved cousin.

"I will visit you, I promise," Milly said with a slightly strained smile. "I am going home first though, Clara. It's time I did; I've been away for four years now; a visit is long overdue." And I need to face up to what I have hidden from she thought to herself but knew that Clara was aware of some of what she was thinking.

"Long visits," Clara said with feeling.

Milly smiled. She adored her cousin and was convinced of the love and affection that Clara and Edmund shared but, in some ways, it would be torture for Milly to be on the side-lines of their affection. It would almost be like watching what she could have had with another if things had turned out differently; but that one, the man whom she had thought to love and care for until her dying breath had let her down so very cruelly. Returning home would put her inevitably in his circle as well as forcing her to face up to other pain, but she had to do it. She had avoided facing her past for the four years she had been companion to Clara, and it was time to exorcise the demons.

Henry had watched the exchange with interest. He was trained to miss nothing in a person's expression, demeanour or tone of voice, and it seemed from the exchange of the last few minutes there was a lot more to Miss Millicent Holland than he had first presumed.

In some respects it was tempting for Henry to remain in contact with the family to find out a little more about Milly, but then he mentally shook himself. He had a job to do, and if he stayed he was sure the novelty of her would soon wear off; a number of discarded mistresses would attest to that fact; it always happened that way. He could not imagine that an innocent spinster would provide any more entertaining than some of the ladies he had previously chased; no, it was better to leave Miss Holland alone.

*

The party gathered outside on the narrow pavement on Half Moon Street, saying their goodbyes to the happy couple. Edmund handed his wife into his plush carriage, refitted for their wedding trip. He closed the door behind him, and the couple waved as the carriage pulled away, the small party remaining on the pavement until the carriage had turned the corner.

"Would you like to join us in a walk through Hyde Park, my lord?" Charles asked cheerfully. He was eager to join his sweetheart on her afternoon promenade.

"No. Thank you, I shall take the opportunity to walk back to Berkeley Square," Henry said pleasantly. He had experienced enough happiness for one day; he had no desire to witness Charles pandering to his chosen one. Young people in love were tedious at best and in most cases sickeningly boring.

"Very well. I hope to see you in White's sometime soon," Charles said easily.

"No doubt," came the uncommitted reply. Henry turned towards Milly, who it was plain to see was keen to return inside the house. "Miss Holland, I hope to see you at one of the entertainments before the end of the season. You are an exquisite dance partner, and I would hope to have the pleasure again soon." He took Milly's hand and placed a kiss on it, enjoying that she wore no gloves and knowing that it would increase her discomfort.

Milly's breath caught in the back of her throat at Henry's touch, and she stiffened, wanting to pull her hand away but, because of propriety, not able too. "My lord," she said stiffly and curtsied at his bow, turning immediately towards the house. She was not going to remain where he could see her state of tumult; he was the type of man to take pleasure out of it.

She would have been surprised to know that her reaction was enough of a rejection to the confident Earl that it was he who walked away with his mind agitated about the prim Miss Holland.

Chapter 2

Henry was to avoid society for the next few weeks, but it was not done purposely. He would have liked to dance with the pretty Milly, who tormented his thoughts when he allowed anything other than the business he had to do enter his mind.

He had not appreciated just how much information Edmund had discovered by visiting the less salubrious venues in society, so now with Edmund on his wedding trip and refusing to work as a spy on his return, it was down to Henry to fill the gap until someone else could be recruited.

The one advantage to spending the evening in venues where he now found himself, was that he did not need to be quite as pleasing as the hosts in civilised entertainments demanded. Convenient in his present mood.

He was currently engaged in a card party in a venue that could only be described as a bawdyhouse. It was less respectable than Mrs Langtree's, which Edmund and Charles had regularly frequented, if such places could be classed by levels of respectability, but it guaranteed a different kind of gentleman, in which Henry was very interested.

The house was relatively clean, and the beer flowed freely, stronger alcohol available for a price. Most of the visitors preferred the cheaper beer, but Henry had opted for a wine of dubious claret. He sat with three other men, playing five-card Loo. He had been sent a note directing him to this specific establishment by another operative, suggesting that he might be able to find out some information about the elusive Joshua Shambles.

The man had gone to ground since that night on the beach at Charles' estate. Five men had been killed in the fracas, thankfully none of them Henry's. Four other men had hanged once a very short trial had taken place, and four others had been transported as a result of a second trial, saving their own lives by giving information on their counterparts and the other landings that had occurred on the same night.

The operation had been held up as a huge success; one of the largest co-ordinated secret attacks on England had been foiled, and Henry was a hero in the eyes of the Home Office. Unfortunately, the role of spy was looked down on by most people, so his work and accolades went unnoticed by the population in general, and he continued to be seen purely as a rake about town.

One of the criminals, but not the main ringleader, was Joshua Shambles, a man whom Henry had a particular reason to find, but Shambles had gone to ground, and no one seemed to know where he was. He had been injured in the fracas, but the extent of his injuries was unknown. Henry was desperate to find out what had happened to Joshua, hence his attendance at a seedy bawdyhouse.

The game was going reasonably well, but they were interrupted by one of the girls of the house, sitting uninvited on Henry's knee.

"Are you not tired of this game, mister?" she asked, wriggling on his knee provocatively.

Henry smiled at the young woman. She looked older than her years, but she was not unattractive. He snaked his free hand around her waist and pulled her closer to him. "What would you suggest I do instead?" he asked with one of his dazzling smiles. He was used to being a draw for ladies of all characters, most were attracted to his dark hair and laughing hazel eyes. If they had known what coldness lay beneath the surface, they would have run in the opposite direction.

"Come, spend some time with me," she offered, leaning in to kiss him.

Henry welcomed the kiss while his co-players looked on amused. The young woman pulled away from him; too many kisses without payment were bad for business. As she moved she noticed a frown on her chosen one's face. "What's wrong?" she asked. "You can have more if you want. You can have anything you want, mister."

Henry focused on her words. He had enjoyed the kiss; any man in his prime would appreciate a young, attractive woman on his knee, but something had happened during the kiss. A pair of clear grey eyes had flitted into his mind's eye and, as a result, the moment had been spoiled. They had looked at him with fire before pooling with tears and as suddenly as the image had appeared his ardour was gone.

He was annoyed with himself; he was mooning over an old maid when there was a young, willing and very able girl in his lap. He moved in for another kiss, but his mouth went uncomfortably dry before his lips touched the girl's, and he groaned, pushing her gently off his knee.

He reached inside his waistcoat pocket and took out a few coins. "Here, take these. Maybe another night but not tonight," he said roughly, his smile gone.

The girl pouted in disappointment, although she was happy with the amount of coins she had been given. It was uncommon to have such an attractive specimen within their walls; she had wanted to enjoy her evening rather than being forced to pretend enjoyment with some of the other men who frequented the establishment. Realising that the moment had passed, she moved off to find another, more willing, partner. Time was money after all.

Henry was tiring of being affected by one kiss and from a woman who had less life experience than he had in a month! The whole situation was ridiculous in the extreme. He ordered another bottle of wine; the memories would be deadened one way or another.

*

The man walked through the streets, his collar up, his shoulders hunkered down against the night air. That is what anyone passing him would have presumed; the reality was that Joshua Shambles did not like looking anyone in the eye these days.

He had managed to escape from the beach in Dorset through sheer determination. Charles had lashed out, his knife in his hand and had sliced a gash across Joshua's cheek. It had been unexpected, Joshua never presuming once that the young fop would ever fight back; he would have a constant reminder of that lapse of judgement for the remainder of his days.

The scream he had uttered had been caused by the pain ripping through his cheek, and he had stumbled backwards. Everything had happened fast: the light extinguished and a gunshot went off. He had stumbled to the opening of the cave a few steps behind Claude close enough to see Claude sending one of the nobs sprawling across the sand with one of his punches.

Joshua had used the diversion to head towards the cliff path. There was enough moonlight to see the excise man at the bottom of the path, and he had climbed up to the pathway from the beach, avoiding the officer. It had cost him greatly to remain quiet and move carefully when all he wanted to do was roll on the ground and writhe in agony, but he realised his life was in the balance. If he was caught there was no doubt he would hang.

Keeping to the shadows he had headed down the drive of the house, heading inland. It was clear from the lights appearing in the house that the commotion was waking its residents. The explosion on the beach even made Joshua pause; things were not going as planned, and the sooner he left the coast behind the better.

He had almost collapsed as daylight approached. He saw a farm cart trundling down the lane he was walking. He had to keep away from the main turnpike lest he be spotted by one of the excise men. It would be common knowledge by now that he was injured. The blood on his clothing would cause suspicion in the most gullible of minds.

He waved the cart to a halt and held onto the side of it for support. "I've been robbed, sir. I need help," he uttered before falling to the ground in a faint.

When he awoke, he was in a bed. The straw mattress was not the most comfortable he had slept on, but it was better than any prison cell would have supplied. He was able to spin a convincing story to the farmer and his wife, who listened with horror at his tale. Seven miles inland, they had not heard anything about what had happened on the Dorset beach the previous evening, and it was likely it would be weeks before they did.

They tried to persuade him to have a doctor called for, but he refused. Looking in the mirror, he could see the horror that was his face and knew that without help the scar would look horrific for the rest of his days. It was a sacrifice he would have to make. A doctor moved around the area far more than two peasant farmers did, and he would be at risk of discovery.

He stayed with the farmer and his wife for two weeks; when he could move around without too much pain, it was time to move on. He paid them for their kindness to him and left them, promising to let them know how he fared while knowing full well he would never be in touch with them again.

Travelling slowly and mainly at night, it took days before he arrived in London. There he had to arrange for someone to visit his lodgings in the dead of night and retrieve his worldly goods. Setting up a room in an even more undesirable area of London had been necessary. All pretence of being a gentleman who had fallen on hard times was gone. He now looked like the rogue he was.

Time had passed before he made contact with those who had been in on the organisation of the operation for landing French assassins on English soil. Everyone was laying low whilst the furore and searches were going on as a result of some of the men talking.

He had found out that Claude had killed himself by causing the explosion on the beach. Joshua had some sympathy with that; the man probably could see how things were unfolding and did not wish to hang. Most of Joshua's acquaintances were now either swinging from the gallows or had been transported. It was a dark time for Joshua.

The whole situation was made worse by the fact that he had heard about the wedding of Clara and Edmund and was fully aware of when Charles was to marry his sweetheart. Joshua was totally committed to helping the French to gain the upper hand, but he was determined as part of that he was going to wreak revenge on those who had foiled his plans.

There was no likelihood that Joshua's determination would mellow as time passed. Every time he saw someone new, and they recoiled at his scar, he would grit his teeth and reaffirm his promise of vengeance. Someone was going to pay for what had happened to him.

*

As Henry walked through the dark streets, making his way back to Berkeley Square, he silently fumed. There seemed to be no trace of Joshua. The man could not have disappeared, and he certainly needed to go out in some form of society or other. He was convinced he was somewhere in London.

Henry had to work out a way of expanding the search. He could not do it all himself; he would not be welcome at some of the places Joshua could be frequenting; even Edmund with his previous dissolute behaviour would fail to gain entry in some establishments in London that could hold needed information.

He needed all operatives to be able to recognise who they were looking for. National security was at risk. He needed to come up with some sort of description for the wanted man. It was the only way to track him down, showing those who sought Shambles clearly who Joshua was; only then could he be found.

And Henry was determined that Shambles *would* be found.

Chapter 3

Henry approached Charles at the Wilson's ball. He had finally thought of a brilliant idea that would give him the opportunity to find Joshua. Unfortunately, it would require putting himself in the company of Milly. Even more unfortunately, he found himself much too eager to see the termagant again. He was disturbed at the force of the need he felt when he thought of her.

He consoled himself that he was doing this for King and country, but on both counts, it was more for himself. No one knew the real reason he had started on his quest. To admit it to anyone else was unthinkable; he would open himself up to ridicule in regards to both situations, so he continued on his erroneous mission.

"Baker! How the devil are you?" Henry greeted the young man.

"Very well, my lord!" Charles smiled in response. "More so now I have only a week to wait until I am married."

"Most would dread the union—no more freedom," Henry said somewhat mockingly.

"I've had enough freedom to last me for the rest of my life!" Charles said with feeling. "I'm much happier at the thought of spending my days making my sweet girl happy!"

Henry masked his true expression, keeping the false smile firmly in place. Another one becomes a smitten fool, he thought before continuing. "I was hoping for a dance with your cousin, but don't seem to be able to find her. Is she unwell?"

"Milly? No! She has a strong constitution that one! Nothing fazes her. She's keeping house for me before the wedding, but has expressed a desire to stay at home. I think she is missing Clara's company."

"Oh, I see." Henry knew exactly what had upset Milly's equilibrium; she was clearly not quite as controlled as her cousin thought, but for some strange reason the action had also upset his own, so he wisely kept his thoughts to himself. "I have a favour to ask of her; perhaps I should call on you both tomorrow?"

Charles' face dropped. "I'm expected at the Beresford's house at a damned early hour, my lord," Charles said, his voice lowered. "I'm meeting with Mr Beresford to go through a few queries he has about the wedding. It all seems a lot of bother over nothing to me."

Henry smiled in genuine amusement. So much for indulging his bride to be; Charles was already bored with wedding preparations. "I'll still call on Miss Holland; it would be a pleasure to see her again."

Charles did not think to ask what favour an Earl would want from his spinster cousin and was soon further distracted by the beautiful Miss Beresford and her golden curls, blue eyes and tinkling laugh. Henry moved away as soon as was polite; he really had no idea why men were attracted to such slips of girls. He would be bored with such a chit in five minutes, and a tinkling laugh made him seriously think of strangulation.

*

The impeccably dressed Henry was led into the drawing room in number six Half Moon Street at the end of morning calls. Milly's colour heightened at his entrance, and Henry's smile widened as he saw her discomfort. "I take it your cousin did not advise you of my intention to pay a call this morning?" he asked drily.

"No! He didn't, but please be seated, my lord." Milly sat down after curtseying and busied herself with making a cup of tea for her guest.

"I was saddened not to have the opportunity to dance with you last night; I know dancing is a pleasure you enjoy."

Milly flushed. "I do, but I find it preferable to miss the evening altogether rather than watch from the chaperones area."

"But you are no longer a chaperone."

"I'm no longer a debutante either. The chaperone area, or the wallflower benches, they are both effectively the same. I watch, not partake." There was no resentment in Milly's tone, just an acceptance of her great age; at eight and twenty it was very unlikely her company would be sought out by anyone wishing to dance. In any entertainment the hosts always ensured that the younger, more lively in society were in attendance to ensure a successful evening. Milly had not been considered part of that set for some time.

"Matches are made even at the end of a season, Miss Holland," Henry could not resist verbally prodding her just a little.

Milly laughed; it was not a tinkle like Miss Beresford's but a real laugh of amusement, which made Henry smile. "Have you noticed the unmarried ladies at the end of a season, my lord?"

"Obviously not in the respect that you have. Tell me more."

"There is a look of desperation in their eyes while they assess the poor souls they'd have rejected at the start of the season. One can almost see the thought processes as they try to decide whether to accept an undesirable proposal or risk another season. Their dilemma is almost palpable."

"Oh, Miss Holland! You are a delight! This is exactly why we get on so well; we have similar levels of cynicism."

Milly stopped smiling. "I would hope not, my lord. And as I recall, we don't get on well. I, for one, am thankful our views are completely at odds with each another."

Henry was stung by her cool tone; he had really been enjoying her company. "I see; well, in that case I shall stick to what I came here for in the first place."

"I would appreciate that."

Henry could not but admire her matter-of-fact tone. "I recall your drawing ability from the sketches you showed me during our time in Dorset, and I wondered if you would do a sketch for me?"

Milly recalled with a blush the one time she had thought Henry was a decent man and not the unfeeling beast she now considered him. He had warned her to keep one of her drawings a secret because she had inadvertently drawn two of the men who were intent on using the beach for illegal activity. He had seemed so concerned for her safety, but now it seemed the reality was that he had not wished his planned ambush to suffer any set-back.

"What would you wish me to do?"

"Mr Shambles has gone to ground since that night," Henry started. "We've done everything we can to try to find him but to no avail."

"Would it not be best to leave things as they are then?" Milly asked. "Surely if he is hiding, he won't try to do anything again?"

"If only that where the case," Henry responded. "No, he will be up to his old tricks soon enough. I need to find him before he can arrange something on the scale of last time. If they'd have succeeded, it could have caused death on our streets, and we don't want the nation in a state of panic with Napoleon already running riot all over Europe."

"What can I do?" Milly read the papers; the chance of an invasion was a very real fear for most of the population. Each success Napoleon achieved seemed to overshadow his defeats. Everyone was being urged to help in the fight against the tyrant, and Joshua Shambles was heavily involved.

"Can you produce a drawing of Joshua? I know your ability; I've seen it and, if you can reproduce his likeness, I can have it printed and circulated far and wide. I believe it's our best chance of tracking him down."

Milly thought for a moment. She did have a good memory and could produce a picture of Joshua; his scowling face was imprinted on her memory, but it would mean more contact with Henry, and that would certainly upset her equanimity.

She sighed; there was no choice really; she owed it to her country if nothing else. "I will do as you ask. Could I see the printing process though? I admit to being curious as to how it would be done."

"I can't see why not," Henry said with a small smile. He had been convinced for a moment she was going to turn him down, so he was ready to agree to almost anything to gain her co-operation.

"If you give me a few days, my lord, I should have some sketches for you to choose from."

"Thank you, Miss Holland. I appreciate your help. I've no need to remind you that this needs to be carried out in the utmost secrecy?"

"I will not utter a word of our conversation or my task," Milly assured him. Even for one who never trusted anybody, Henry was completely sure of Milly's word. She was probably the only person in the world he trusted; an honour she would never be made aware of.

*

It was four long days before Milly saw Henry once more. She could not have refused him anything when it was to do with the country's security, but she was a bundle of nerves at the thought of seeing him again. She was disgusted with herself; he half irritated her, half made her want to swoon at his feet like a silly debutante. He was so handsome with the ruggedness of his square jaw and long nose, the high cheekbones and shrewd hazel eyes. His features were finished to perfection by the dazzling smile he could bestow when the mood took him. She could honestly say she had never seen features made to so perfectly complement each other. It was very distracting.

She could also remember the feel of his lips when he had taken her kisses. Oh yes, she had given them willingly, but he had taken what he wanted and then pushed her away. In some respects it had been worse than the first time she had been pushed away, but she suspected her perspective might change when she had to face up to that rejection when she returned home. A long absence had probably lessened that pain.

Henry was shown into the drawing room, noticing with pleasure Milly's figure, visible in her light cotton day gown. The dress she wore was emerald green, not as dark as a woman of her age could wear but deeper than that of a girl in her first seasons. It suited her colouring, which was enhanced because of her blush. She was quite tall, which was attractive to a man who usually stood a head above most of his acquaintances. She was slim; there was no widening of her girth even though she had passed the first bloom of youth. She had a pretty face rather than a beautiful one, but it was her eyes that seemed to look all the way to his soul that perturbed him and haunted his dreams. He had never been drawn to anyone in his life before, and he was fighting the feelings with all his might; whether he was being successful or not depended on what excuse he used to try and justify his seeking her out.

"I've made a few sketches," Milly started. "I thought it would be best to give you a choice."

"I'm already convinced of your ability to capture a likeness; I'm sure they will all be well executed," Henry replied, honestly.

They were unexpectedly interrupted by Charles. Neither wanted to explain about the drawing, so Charles was served tea by Milly, and the conversation turned to inane topics.

"I was saying to Milly that she should stay on after I've been married. There's no point leaving town when Clara will be passing through sometime afterwards," Charles said, his open manner disclosing issues that Milly would rather have kept private.

"Ah, so the newlyweds return soon, do they?" Henry asked with interest.

"Perhaps, although they haven't sent firm plans yet. I believe their visit, when it is made, will only be of a short duration," Milly said. "They are removing themselves to the Hampshire countryside. Lord Chertsey is still determined to keep Clara out of harm's way."

There was meaning in the words that Henry understood perfectly. "Chertsey was clear that he would not be contacting me again; don't worry your pretty little head, Miss Holland. I'm not able to embroil him in anything he doesn't wish to get involved with."

Milly had bristled at the patronising words but remained calm. "I'm sure you would try, though, so I'm thankful they shan't be staying for long."

"Will you be following them to Hampshire?"

"No. I said I will visit but not yet. I am to return home in four days, the day of Charles' wedding."

"Where do your family live?"

"In Farnham," Milly responded, not wishing this conversation to continue. For some reason the thought of not seeing Henry again perturbed her. If they continued talking about her departure she might betray some of her inner turmoil.

Charles, for once, seemed to sense Milly's discomfort and stood up, hoping to break up the grouping. "Milly, could you give me the reticule you've made for Miss Beresford, please? If Lord Grinstead will excuse me, I'd like to deliver it to her today."

"Of course, I will excuse you," Henry said as Milly stood to leave the room. "If I don't see you before, I wish you every happiness on your marriage."

"Thank you!" Charles said with a bow.

The cousins left Henry alone, but not before Milly had looked astonished at hearing Henry's words. Her reaction left him chuckling as the door was closed behind the departing cousins.

He reached for the drawing book that had been placed at Milly's side ready to show him the pictures. He began to study each picture as he turned the pages. She was good. She had captured Joshua perfectly: the permanent scowl, the too small eyes. Every feature had been reproduced on the paper.

There were five drawings, each of which was as good as the last. Henry reached blank pages and was going to put the book down when absentmindedly he flicked a few of the pages. Seeing a picture towards the end of the book, he went back to look at it.

He was speechless. It was as if he was staring into a looking glass, the likeness of himself was so great. There was no colour on the picture, but it looked as lifelike as any portrait. Then Henry realised something, it was not him really. The expression was softer than any he ever wore; there was a smile on his lips, when he was fully aware he usually pinched his lips together. It was the same with the eyes, they seemed to be amused, and he was rarely amused. No. She had softened him. She obviously was not as good as he had thought.

He lay the book down, a little disturbed at the picture he had seen but not about to acknowledge that he had seen it. Milly returned to the room and, although she frowned before picking up the drawing book, her expression betrayed nothing of her suspicion that he had seen the pictures.

Henry chose the picture that was most suitable and promised to call on her two days hence. They were both to go to the local printers.

When Henry had left the room, Milly let the book slip out of her hands with a groan. She would have died with shame if he had seen the portrait of himself. She had been so foolish, letting her heart rule her head when she had been drawing.

She had to remind herself that he no longer looked at her in such a gentle way. Expressions like she had reproduced had only been visible when he was fooling them all into thinking he was a man intent only on having fun instead of being the spy he was, determined to use whomever crossed his path to achieve his aim.

She would have been reassured to realise that later in the day Henry would dwell on that picture. He tried to push away the feeling that it would be appealing if, for once, someone could see him as a being with a heart and soul. Only he knew he was a lost cause and longing for something that could never be, did no one any good.

Chapter 4

Milly dressed with care. Of course she did not wish to impress the printer, however clever she thought the skill. It all had to do with her muddled feelings about Henry. She dressed in a cerulean blue day dress. Sometimes this particular colour did not wear well, turning into a greener hue, which did not really suit Milly's complexion; but thankfully the material was of a good quality, and it set off the grey in her eyes to perfection. A delicate grey spencer finished off the outfit, again perfect for enhancing the colour of her eyes.

Milly grimaced at herself in the looking glass, she should be over such vanity at her age but, as she had learned once before, it was all about appearance, and somehow she had the impression that Henry would be exactly the type of person who thought more of how something was presented than of true substance. That in itself should have her running from him, but she was uncharacteristically drawn to him. In some respects it made the past easier to bear. That her heart had not been completely shattered was reassuring. She was under no illusion that she would find someone to spend the rest of her life with, but the way her heart responded to Henry always gave her a nugget of hope that, at some point, she would meet a decent man.

Henry smiled and bowed when Milly entered the hall at Half Moon Street. "You look very well this morning, Miss Holland. I hope the printing press does your pictures justice."

"As long as you are satisfied with the result, I'm sure it will please me. Thankfully, I'm not dependent on the quality as you are, my lord."

They set off in Henry's carriage. Normally Milly would have preferred to walk, although it was perfectly respectable travelling in the carriage, she was fully aware of being confined with a notorious rake. She cursed her heightened colour and tried to maintain her aloof demeanour.

Henry watched Milly closely as they travelled together. She was such a contradictory mixture that she fascinated him. He could see the struggle she was undergoing, and he almost wanted to ease her torment. If he were so inclined he could drag her onto his knee, and he was fairly sure that she would kiss him as she had the last time. The thought of that kiss made him a little uncomfortable, and he moved on the seat, trying to counteract the physical reaction that thinking of her kisses did to him.

They arrived at the printers in good time and stepped out of the carriage. Henry offered his arm and Milly placed her gloved hand on it. Neither openly reacted to the feeling of being in contact with each other, but both were moved by the sensation.

The building was in a row of similar businesses. The noise of the machines could be heard as a rumble in the background. Milly smiled at Henry; she was excited about seeing her drawing turned into something else, and the noises seemed to draw her in, promising all manner of unknown experiences.

They walked through the door and were immediately greeted by a portly gentleman, wearing a thick cloth apron that showed years of wear. He smiled at them, introduced himself and took them through a room at the back. The whole area seemed to be filled with large machines. Men were working at every station, the clatter of the mechanical movements filling the room to an ear-splitting level.

They were led to a smaller room in which the number of machines were fewer, and not all were working, making the sound more bearable.

"Here we are, m'lud," he said with pride. "This is our new lithograph machine. She's a beauty and performs well."

"How does it work?" Milly asked, curious to see the machine in action.

"It's wonderfully simple really, Miss," the printer answered. "We use a lot of different processes to get the block perfect to use and the image to stay on the block. To tell you the basics Miss, the picture m'lud supplied is copied with a crayon onto this limestone block. The grease from the crayon sticks to the limestone and, as you'll see, however many times we use it, the picture will still remain perfect. It's really all about oil and water; no more complicated than that."

"Fascinating," Milly said genuinely interested.

"Let me show you what I mean, Miss." The printer became all business as he showed Milly the limestone block with the picture of Joshua on it. She was impressed at the level of reproduction on the block, the printer making her smile when he admitted that the picture was traced from her original drawing. They both watched as water was applied to the block and then ink to an inking slab, rolling it out with a leather inking roller. He then rolled the roller on the limestone block and, when he was satisfied with the coverage, he placed a sheet of paper over the image, something that he explained spread the weight of the block evenly. The block was then forced through the printing press, and the printer carefully removed the paper, showing a perfect mirror image of Joshua's face.

"That's unbelievable!" Milly said in true appreciation.

"It's very clever and makes a good print. We'll have these ready for you within the hour, m'lud," the printer said, turning to Henry who had remained quiet throughout the lesson. He had been happy to enjoy watching Milly's unaffected interest in the process.

"I shall return shortly afterwards then," Henry said before indicating to Milly that they should leave.

"Thank you for showing me how it's printed. I can see there is more expertise to the process than you have admitted, but you do make it seem so simple. It's almost an hypnotic procedure to watch, which is very arrogant of me, as you clearly work extremely hard. I'm very grateful that you allowed us to interrupt your working day. Good morning to you," Milly said, before leaving the room to once more pass through the noisy printing room.

"Thank you, Miss," the printer responded, a little overwhelmed at the sincere words offered. They left him standing with his chest a little more puffed out than usual.

She blinked when she vacated the building, the noise and smells a little overwhelming.

"So has your curiosity been satisfied, Miss Holland?" Henry asked with a smile.

"Oh yes! It was fascinating; thank you for allowing me to accompany you."

"I think you made a lifelong friend in there," Henry teased, nodding his head to the building, as he handed her into the carriage.

Milly smiled. "I only told the truth."

"In such a way that it charmed him completely!" Henry said with a smile as he seated himself in the carriage. For once he was not being cynical; she had charmed the printer, and it was done with such sincerity he could not criticise her for it.

Milly laughed quietly, pleased at the teasing.

"Miss Holland, if you've no objection I'd like to take you to a little tea shop that I know of not too far away from here. If you are amenable, I can collect the finished pictures before returning you to Half Moon Street."

Milly's first reaction was to refuse, but then she realised that this was going to be the last time they met before she returned home. The thought of home filled her with dread, but pushing aside her melancholy she smiled and agreed. One treat before she left London was not going to hurt her grieving heart any further she reasoned as the carriage made its way to the tea shop.

They were seated in the window, able to watch the busy street. Henry ordered far too many cakes, and Milly laughed when he insisted on her trying every one.

"Has my cousin told you of my sweet tooth?" Milly asked with a smile at the wide array of cakes on the table.

"No, she kept your secret. I'm glad I ordered so many, you must try them all!"

"My dancing days are over, my lord; you shall be sending me home with a need to walk the width and breadth of the town to wear off all these cakes!"

Henry smiled, enjoying the relaxed look and laughing grey eyes. "If I ever hear of a lady carving a path from one end of Farnham to the other, I shall know immediately who they are talking about."

"You must eat more," Milly said, unconsciously pushing a plate of cake towards him and handing him a fork. She blushed at Henry's heated stare, realising she had overstepped polite behaviour; it was not her role to fuss over him in such a way. She busied herself by pouring more tea.

"Who is at home to greet you?" Henry asked, changing the subject to spare her blushes, not realising Milly was as reluctant at speaking about her home as she was at flirting with him.

"My mother. My two younger brothers are at school," Milly said quietly.

"Your father?"

"Died a few years ago," Milly acknowledged.

"I know Farnham a little; I visited once some time ago. I remember Castle Street and the castle but very little else." Henry's tone was easy but, as always, he was watching her with interest.

"We moved to the centre of town after my father died. It is a pretty town; the market fills Castle Street every week, which I always liked to watch from the window. I enjoyed the hustle and bustle it brought."

So there was no money in the family, Henry mused silently. There was usually only one reason a family moved after a death, and that was purely based on finances. It probably explained why she was still single; if there was no dowry, it usually did not matter how pretty the young woman was; there was always going to be someone richer, although not necessarily as pretty or entertaining. Those attributes were considered secondary when considering a wife by most of the *ton*.

"Your mother must have missed you. I believe you have been some time with your cousins?"

"Yes, more than four years. I joined them soon after my father died; it suited everyone as it was not long after my aunt had died, and I took on the official role of chaperone to my cousin," Milly explained. Oh, how one could hide so much in so few words! But long may it remain hidden she thought privately.

Henry continued to be charming until it was time to leave. He left Milly seated in his carriage while he completed his business transaction with the printer and then gave instructions to return his companion to her home. Surprisingly, he had enjoyed his afternoon out but, just as Milly did, he realised they would not cross paths again.

He sighed as they travelled through the streets of London. He needed to do something that had been niggling away at him for weeks now, and the action would not come naturally to him.

"Miss Holland, I have an apology to make," he started.

"Oh?"

"Yes, that blasted night in Dorset is haunting me for a number of reasons. One of the reasons involves you."

Milly immediately flushed a deep red. "I feel it would be better for both of us if we don't mention that evening, my lord," she said, not wishing to resurrect the feelings that were already difficult enough to suppress. It was a shame to cast a cloud over proceedings when the afternoon had been so pleasant.

"I behaved like a complete scoundrel," Henry said quietly.

"You did," Milly admitted.

Henry chuckled. "Yes, I did! I'm sorry I reacted so cruelly; you didn't deserve it, and I wish I could take back the words I uttered."

"What did you say that was so wrong? I would not be brave if faced with what happened that evening, and I'm fully aware that I couldn't protect myself. You were right: a pencil is little weapon against people who are going to be hanged if caught," Milly said fairly. She had already admitted to herself that his words had been a correct assessment of her character.

Henry moved across the carriage, so he was seated at Milly's side and took her gloved hand in his. "I was inexcusably harsh. I was angry with myself; I *had* been dismissive about the dangers to those around me, and there could have been many more deaths than there were. I was hiding from everything because I knew it was my fault and then you came running around that corner and tore a strip off me. I wasn't ready to accept it then, but every word you uttered was true."

"It was a hard night for everyone involved," Milly acknowledged, looking down at her hand being clasped in his large one.

Henry watched the gentle Milly as her colour heightened. What was it about her that made him long to put his arms around her and protect her from the rest of the world? He had never felt that about anyone else—except one, but he could never allow himself to dwell on those memories; they were a physical pain, barely suppressed. For the first time, since meeting Milly, he had found someone who made him feel warm inside, warmer than the ice block he usually felt.

He took one of Milly's curls and curled it through his free fingers. "I could so easily kiss you now like I did on that night," he said with a smile at Milly's surprised expression at his touch.

"You pushed me away," Milly said quietly. She wanted him to kiss her so much she ached to lean into him, but it was no use. His kisses were a risk to her reputation and she could not act so foolishly for a second time.

"You should have run from me then, and you should run from me now. I'm not a good man, Miss Holland."

"I'm sure you are being too harsh on yourself, my lord."

"Am I?" Henry asked gruffly. He could tell her tales that would shock her and convince her never to look at him the way she sometimes did. He was a fool for needing her good opinion and decided to take control of the situation. "Your kisses weren't that of an innocent," he said, reverting back to his usual persona and voicing the words that had bothered him since he had touched her lips.

Milly looked pained, once more reminded of a time she would rather forget. "I have kissed before." There was no point in lying.

An expression of anger crossed Henry's face which surprised her. It would have puzzled her further if she had realised how much Henry was trying to control his feelings at the thought that someone else had experienced her first tentative kisses.

They were disturbed by the coach coming to a halt, and Henry cursed that they had arrived at Half Moon Street. He bent forward and kissed Milly lightly on the lips before a footman opened the carriage door. There was no opportunity to lengthen the kiss as he wished to.

Milly used her free hand and, for a second, she threw caution to the wind and cupped Henry's cheek in her hand. "Goodbye, my lord. Stay safe," she whispered before moving to the carriage door. She reached out and let the footman help her onto the pavement.

Not looking back, Milly entered the house. This time he had kissed her, not reacting in anger as he had on that first fateful night, but in some ways, he had hurt her just as much. She would be returning home with so much longing in her heart that it would be difficult to function, but any girlish dreams were crushed when she heard the sound of the carriage pulling away and travelling down the street. Women like her did not attract men like Lord Grinstead, of that she was completely sure.

Chapter 5

Farnham, Surrey.

Milly watched the carriage leave with a heavy heart. Charles and his new wife had kindly altered their wedding trip in order that they could deposit her safely at home. Charles had again tried to persuade her to stay in London, waiting for Clara's return, but she was sure that coming home was the right thing to do. Things had changed, as she had expected them to do, always presuming that Clara would marry, and so now she had to take control of her own future.

Turning back into the small townhouse Milly closed the door and set her shoulders. There was nothing to gain in postponing the inevitable. She entered the front room of the house, and her mother looked at her in disgust.

"I hope you've earned enough to pay for your keep while you're here. I can't be expected to pay for you!" The older woman said. She was as tall as Milly, but thinner; some would describe her as too thin. Her eyes were the same as her daughter's but could not have been more different in the way they looked at the world. Mrs Holland was a woman who perceived herself to be hard done by; she took no responsibility for the way her life had unfolded, expecting everyone around her to shoulder the blame and at the same time provide for her. She had been a flighty young woman who had married a foolish man. Their lifestyle had ruined them and, from then on, Mrs Holland had been unreasonably bitter and twisted about life and what she thought was owed to her.

"I was a guest of Clara's not a paid member of staff," Milly said quietly. She was relieved the onslaught had not started whilst Charles had been present; her cousin had done so much for her family, she did not wish him to witness her mother's bitterness.

"So, you're as penniless as you left then!"

Milly had been given an allowance, as well as her food, board and clothing for all the years she had lived with her cousins. She could have told her mother she had managed to save some money, although it was not enough to consider herself rich. It would be just enough to tide her over until she sought a paid position.

"I shall be applying to be a companion to someone else as soon as a position is advertised," Milly explained dully. "I'm hoping not to encroach on your hospitality for too long." It hurt Milly and her siblings that her parent saw her three children as burdens to be got rid of.

"I should hope not! I can't afford luxuries that you'd be used too, swanning around London like you had no cares in the world!"

"I escorted Clara, that is all."

"I've hardly two ha'pennies to rub together. You could have sent me any spare funds you had."

"I didn't have any," Milly responded, consoling herself that she was not unreasonable in lying to her parent. "Charles pays for everything you need, Mother. I know you have no financial worries; he makes sure of that."

It was true; the kind-hearted Charles had stepped in when Milly's father died and left them all facing ruin. It had been shocking how fast the creditors had emerged, almost as soon as her father had taken his last breath, but Milly could not really blame them; her parents had lived frivolous, expensive lives. Charles had committed to paying for her two brothers to be sent to school; Milly had been sent to live with Clara, and her mother had received enough funds to live in a small house in the centre of town. Mrs Holland hated the fact that she had fallen down the social scale so much and blamed everyone apart from herself and her deceased husband.

Milly was the main one of her children who her mother unfairly blamed for her straitened circumstances. "Mrs Connor visits me regularly," Mrs Holland said, finally starting on the topic of conversation that had been inevitable but dreaded by Milly.

"I hope she is well," Milly responded, feeling dead inside.

"She will be as she is living in the big house, which should have been yours!"

"It was never going to be mine once father died, and the reality of our situation became clear." It had been hard to grieve for someone who had acted in such a selfish way, disregarding the impact on his children and their futures. Milly would never forget the tears of her brothers as they berated themselves for not realising what was happening. She had tried to comfort them; there was a large age gap between the siblings, the ones who had been born between Milly and her brothers not surviving the first months of pregnancy, which contributed to the feelings of bitterness already developing within her mother.

"You should have done something to secure the engagement! You just sat by and watched him walk out of your life!" Mrs Holland snapped. She looked at her daughter with disgust for failing in her duty to secure a good match.

"Mr Connor wanted nothing to do with me or this family once he realised there would be no dowry after father's death," Milly said. She had not had to utter the words for four years, but they still stirred up feelings of the complete betrayal she had experienced when hearing them from the man she had loved.

"You were engaged!"

"And he withdrew the offer, facing the scandal of that action, rather than the lack of funds. He knew full well that we couldn't sue for breach of promise." It had been the worst time of Milly's life, even worse than losing her father, if she were honest. A death stirred sympathy, a broken engagement caused gossip and unkind speculation. Especially, as it was rarely heard of for a gentleman to call off the engagement from a lady.

"You could have used the word compromise," Mrs Holland said, not for the first time.

"And completely ruin my reputation and either have a husband who despised me, or an abandonment issue with which to contend and even more gossip to deal with!" Milly responded tartly. She sighed. "I will soon have a paid position, Mother, and be off your hands again. I'm sure it will only take a short time."

"In the meantime, I'm living in this hovel when I could have been living with you in the grand house that *they* now live in!"

Milly let out a breath; her mother would never accept anything other than she was ill-used; she would always abhor the house she lived in. Admittedly, it was not as grand a house as they had all lived in until Mr Holland died, but the reality was that they would have probably lost that house because of the debt anyway if he had not died so suddenly. The death had purely hastened the inevitable and given Mr Connor the opportunity to renege on his offer.

Mrs Holland hated her little house. It was in a good part of town and although it had only two downstairs rooms in addition to the kitchen area, there was a pleasant upstairs drawing room and three bedrooms. Thanks to Charles, Mrs. Holland was able to afford a cook who came in each day, a housemaid who worked daily and a man of all works who visited twice a week to carry out all the tasks the maid and cook could not or were not prepared to do.

For a lady living alone, this should have been enough; Milly was aware of many people who did not live in such luxury, but Charles had insisted on providing for his relation, and Mrs Holland would never have considered the burden of her needs on Charles' funds. So she had moved from her far grander home on the outskirts of Farnham to the centre of town and had not stopped complaining since.

The bombardment on Milly by her parent continued until she sought refuge outdoors. There were still some people she considered friends in the town where she had grown-up in and she visited them without her mother in tow to dampen the mood.

One such friend, the now Mrs Sarah Hastings greeted Milly with open affection after reading the card she had supplied to the footman. Sarah was the same age as Milly, securing a very early marriage and now lived very comfortably with her husband and her increasing brood.

"So, how many children is it now? It must be double figures!" Milly teased with a smile as she took a sip of Jasmine tea.

"You know full well how many there are, as they all eagerly await for the post to arrive on birthdays, to see what treats Aunt Milly has sent, although sometimes I admit I forget how many I've got myself!"

Sarah laughed. "Eight darlings and one more to arrive in a few months."

"It's nice to be able to offer my congratulations in person," Milly responded.

"I thought we had a house full when we reached five, but it appears that we are to be blessed with a large family. The nursery can get very noisy, but I do like seeing them all happy."

"I can imagine that life is never dull."

"No, not at all, especially when one comes down with something. My children love to share everything, illnesses included! The nanny is a saint, thankfully, and soon the eldest boys will be going to school; that should help to keep her sane!"

"I love receiving your letters, and I expect them to continue when I leave for pastures new."

"I wondered what you intended to do. I wish you would stay near Farnham; it has been too many years since I've seen you," Sarah said with feeling. The women had been inseparable as they had grown, and each had missed the other's company over the last few years.

"It is, but I'm afraid I could not stay with mother; she is not happy that I've returned, already lamenting about it for more than an hour," Milly said with feeling. Sarah was the only person that Milly could be honest with.

"You poor thing. I don't suppose you have seen the Connors yet, have you?"

"No. I have that delight to come," Milly groaned.

"She, especially, glides around town as if she owns the place!" Sarah harrumphed in disgust.

Milly smiled. "As one of the wealthiest families in town, I suppose she does in a way."

"I wish they'd move away. Every time I see him I want to give him a piece of my mind! Are you not angry with him?"

"After all this time? No! There would be no point in that," Milly said reasonably. "He hurt me, and there is still a wound that hasn't completely healed, I admit. But he gave me the chance to withdraw from the engagement, which would have saved some heartache, only I chose to refuse to do that. I sometimes think I was too stubborn and should have taken the option to call it off."

"I can't blame you for that. You loved him," Sarah said softly.

"But he didn't love me, so perhaps it's for the best," Milly responded stoically. The thought that the man she had been engaged to had not loved her had crushed Milly when the engagement had been broken off but, somewhere over the past few years, Milly had come to terms with the rejection, at a distance at least; whether she would feel the same when faced with him, she had yet to find out.

"I still can't abide the weasel!"

Milly laughed. "Don't make yourself uncomfortable on my account; it isn't worth it, I promise you!"

*

If Milly was hoping for a quiet time at home until she found a position that would see her leaving her home town once again, she had forgotten how demanding her mother was. Having bemoaned Milly's arrival, Mrs Holland then proceeded to insist on Milly's attendance at every invitation she received.

Mrs Holland always tried to be invited out every evening. Her justification was that it was less costly for her to visit than to stay in, anything to save a penny or two. The town was big enough to have sufficient families who were happy to invite such a grateful widow into their midst; none would witness the bitter woman that Milly was subjected too.

It was inevitable that Milly would cross paths with the people she least wanted to meet and, so it was, on the second evening she was in Mr Marshall's drawing room when Mr and Mrs Connor were announced.

Milly was aware there were many eyes looking in her direction, but she maintained her composure, carrying on the conversation she had been enjoying until the announcement was made. She did not look at the newcomers until she was approached by Mrs Connor.

"Miss Holland! So, the rumours are true, and you have returned home," Mrs Connor exclaimed. She was the same age as Milly, and had, in the distant past, shared a friendship of sorts, but that had come to a halt after the death of Mr Holland.

"I have. Good evening, Mrs Connor," Milly said, curtseying and inclining her head slightly in greeting.

"We have enjoyed your letters, full of news; your Mama delighted in reading them to us. You put us to shame, all the gadding about you did in London and Dorset! We must seem positively rustic to you now!"

"Not at all." Milly cringed inwardly that her mother had boasted about what she was doing in London; everyone knew she was there as a companion which made the boasting all the more to be ridiculed by those who chose to and, as in other towns up and down the country, there were many of that type of person filling the drawing rooms.

"You must come by one day and take tea with us. See how the old place has changed!" Mrs Connor said, sensing the discomfort, rather than being able to see it. Milly was determined not to give anything away.

"Thank you."

"My darling Mr Connor, shouldn't Miss Holland come to visit us? She'll be astounded at the change in the house, won't she?"

Mr Connor approached the pair, having the decency to look uncomfortable, but he smiled at Milly, a smile that did not reach his eyes. "Of course, whenever you wish."

"Thank you," Milly responded. It was now more than four years since it had happened, but he had not changed overmuch. His girth was slightly wider, his hair slightly thinner, and the creases a sign of the frowns he normally wore were deeply ingrained, but he was still the first man she had fallen in love with. He was the one she had shared kisses with, had planned a future with, but he had betrayed her.

"You will have to meet my babies," Mrs Connor gushed. Her expression betraying that she was fully aware of what she wanted her words to achieve.

"How many children do you have?" Milly asked politely.

"Three, two girls and a boy. Who would have thought that I would have so many children and you none as yet? I remember you always saying you wanted a large family; well never mind; I'm sure there is still time. My babies are absolute images of their father. It will be as if you are looking back at the past if you see them!"

"I shall look forward to it. Please excuse me; Mrs Hastings is trying to catch my attention," Milly said thankful of an escape.

She approached Sarah with a grimace. "Tell me not everyone could hear every word she uttered."

"I'm afraid so," Sarah muttered with a glare towards Mrs Connor's back. "How utterly insensitive! Although she will have gained no favours by being so openly cruel."

"I think she disguised it quite well; she was all smiles and didn't actually say anything wrong," Milly responded with a sigh. "I should perhaps have stayed with my cousins until I secured a place. I don't seem to be very good at making sensible decisions for myself!"

"Why should you not come home? This has been your home just as long as it has been theirs. It isn't right that you feel unwelcome. Please say you won't visit them."

"I doubt my mother would allow me to avoid an invitation when there is food involved. You know her miserly ways," Milly said with a whisper.

"Yes, but in your old house?"

"I expect that will increase her determination to accept the invitation. Then I can be shown what supposedly could have been mine. I do wish she would accept what happened."

Milly was fully aware of how long Mrs Holland would spend berating her once Milly had seen the inside the house that had once been their home. There had been remonstrations throughout the years, luckily in letter form, preventing their vehemence being quite as strong as it would be face to face. The placid-natured Milly resigned herself to the scolding she would receive. It appeared that even at eight and twenty she was still at the mercy of her mother's disappointment.

When mother and daughter finally returned home, Milly wished her parent good night and sought refuge in her bedchamber. It was a small room, but perfectly adequate for the bed, chest of drawers and chair that filled the room. A screen in the corner shielded the washing bowl and stand. The window looked out over the street, which Milly enjoyed as it allowed her to hear the sounds of the night decreasing as the hours passed before morning heralded the start of another busy day on Castle Street.

As she lay in her bed, Milly pondered the evening. She had thought it would be worse; yes, Mrs Connor's insensitivity, perhaps even gloating, had been hard to bear, but it had not affected her as much as she had expected it too.

In her mind she had remembered him differently, almost as if she had not been worthy of him. She had realised something that she probably should have thought of long before; he was not the perfect specimen she had turned him into; instead he was the man who had treated her shamefully and had transferred his affection so quickly to another. Milly no longer believed he had been seriously attached to her in the first place, and the thought did not upset her the way she expected it to.

She had to admit to surprise that, when she had seen him, her heart did not flutter; she was not rendered breathless, and her eyes did not fill with tears of regret. Those were the reactions that had been expected by probably half the people in the drawing room, but there were no such reactions; in fact any feeling had been lacking; she admitted to herself that seeing him had not moved her at all; oh yes, the situation was embarrassing, and having the life that they had planned out for themselves being described by Mrs Connor as her own was hard to bear, but any regret at the loss of her beau was absent.

It was a strange position to be in when something had been so much a part of her for so long, but she felt a weight lift when she realised she no longer loved him and fell asleep pondering whether her feelings had been anything more than a first infatuation.

Chapter 6

Milly was to be proved correct; when the invitation came, Mrs Holland insisted on accompanying her daughter to take tea with Mrs Connor.

They walked to the manor house they had once called home, taking advantage of the bright afternoon sunshine. Milly looked with interest at the grounds as there was a nugget of curiosity to see her old home and the effects a large dowry had had on it. The gardens had clearly been redesigned; new formal pathways wound their way through what had been grassed areas. People visiting could see some of the dramatic features as soon as they traversed on the driveway, which was clearly planned to impress all new arrivals to the property.

From the outside the house looked the same as it had for centuries, Tudor fronted with later additions kept to the back of the house to avoid spoiling the frontage. Mrs Connor was waiting for them at the doorway, a unique method of greeting someone; she had clearly been watching for their arrival.

"Do come in!" she exclaimed, when they were still a minute from the large wooden doorway. "Welcome to our humble abode!"

The pair were welcomed into the square hallway where, along with relieving them of their bonnets and parasols, Mrs Connor, pointed out every change in furniture and decoration that had taken place since the house had been bought at a very reasonable price to ease the burden of the debts.

"Before we take tea, let me show you the rest of the house! I know you'll be eager to see it!"

Milly smiled, wondering how a hostess' words could be so far from the truth. Milly was curious; that she admitted to herself, but the animosity radiating from her mother did not bode well. The problem was that Milly was fully aware that the ill-feeling was directed at herself rather than their hostess; each step they took into every room would reinforce the fact that her mother believed Milly could have done something to secure Mr Connor. Her mother's belief should have been a compliment, but the reality was it was not.

Eventually, they returned to the morning room, where Mrs Connor bemoaned the lack of morning sunshine in the room, expressing that it would have been better placed in another location, but the room was too small to be put to any better use. Mrs Holland stiffened in her chair, but Milly was relieved to see that she did not utter anything that would cause upset. A pity their hostess did not have the same restraint.

"I hope you think we have improved the house. It was badly in need of repair when we moved in," Mrs Connor babbled. Her brunette curls bouncing around her face as she spoke.

"You have made many changes," Milly answered diplomatically.

"I wanted to pull it down and start again, but Mr Connor was sentimental about the building so, as you can see, I refitted it completely. I've asked Nanny to bring the children down. I just know you will dote on them!"

The three Connor children were dutifully brought in to be paraded before the visitors. Milly smiled at them in welcome and received shy smiles in return. They all seemed a little in awe of their mother and wary of Mrs Holland, who just glared at them.

When Mrs Connor felt that her children had been admired enough, she sent them away to the nurseries far sooner than Milly had expected. "They could join us," Milly said as they prepared to walk in line out of the door.

"Oh no, dear me, no! They have dirty hands, they might touch something. No, no! They are much better in the nursery; we haven't changed that part of the house since we moved here; it is perfectly fine for messy children."

Milly's heart felt heavy at the thought of the children, not important enough to have their rooms refitted, something that had needed to be done even in her own day of using the rooms.

"So are you excited to attend the ball next week?" Mrs Connor asked, forgetting her children as soon as they had left the room.

"I'm not aware of an upcoming ball," Milly responded.

"Why the ball here of course! It's an annual event, isn't it, Mrs Holland? As one of the high families in the area, I think it's important to set the standards for the others in town. Mummy and Daddy pay for it of course; Mr Connor says we are not frittering away our own money when Mummy and Daddy don't need the amount that they have. It will be a wonderful event; the flowers alone will cost over a hundred pounds!"

"It sounds impressive," Milly responded. She inwardly groaned; would the torture never end? She would have to sit with the wallflowers, it was a guarantee; no one would come near her to dance, afraid of upsetting their host. Suddenly the town felt too small.

Mrs Connor continued to express how wonderful her life was and how perfect her husband was. She never stopped in her flow of inane babble; the result being that Milly almost started to pity Mr Connor–almost but not quite.

Eventually, they were allowed to leave with the promise that Mrs Connor would call on them tomorrow with a personal invitation for Milly. She was determined the woman she viewed as her rival would be in attendance on the night that she was the belle of the town.

Mrs Holland was quiet as they started to retrace their steps; both women were drained at being bombarded by such nonstop chatter for so long.

Eventually she sighed. "It should be you organising that ball."

"No, it shouldn't. I would have hated my life to turn out like that," Milly said with feeling.

"What, rather than living as some stranger's companion?" Mrs Holland snapped.

"Mother," Milly sighed. "He broke off the engagement with me. I had no control over the situation. Added to that, we would not have had the same life as he is enjoying now." She was aware that her dowry would not have provided the luxuries that Mrs Connor's dowry had.

"You could have done something! I prefer the country air to being in the centre of town."

"I'm sorry about that, Mother, but let's hope Stephen and Gerald will set-up a home in the country, and you could perhaps live with them," Milly said jovially.

"It is the daughter's role to care for her parents, not the sons! You should have provided better for me!"

As Milly could not have guaranteed that Mr Connor would have agreed with her mother's sentiments even if they had married, she thought it prudent to remain silent on the subject.

*

Milly sat with Sarah, drinking tea, the atmosphere of the house completely different than the one she had visited that morning. In this home the children were free to explore and play when not in lessons or having naps. It meant that the building was constantly noisy, filled with laughter with only the occasional natural tears of childhood being heard.

"It must have been strange to visit after all this time," Sarah said, settling in for a chat.

"It was, but it's been so long now that I didn't feel anything until she said that they hadn't refurbished the nurseries! Those poor children!"

Sarah smiled. "She is all about show and always has been. The children are there to be paraded when appropriate and hidden away for the rest of the time. She is always lecturing me about lack of control over my brood."

Milly laughed. "I know which house I'd rather live in."

"Did you see that dastardly man?"

"No! You must stop that Sarah. It really doesn't matter."

"I know I should be more magnanimous. You are very forgiving, and if you have forgiven him I should be able to as well, but if you'd married him you wouldn't be constantly leaving us." Sarah bemoaned what she saw as the loss of her dearest friend.

"You are very sweet and a dear friend, but I honestly think that, on reflection, we wouldn't have suited. From the little I've heard, he seems to be driven by money; I could never be that way. And from all accounts they are supported a lot by the parents;

again, something that wouldn't have happened if we had married."

"You are more generous in the circumstances than I could be."

"I'm being realistic. And anyway, I'm normally quite happy with my lot; well I was..," Milly started, surprising herself as she realised what her words meant.

"Has coming home upset you so much?" Sarah asked sadly.

"No, it's what I left behind that has upset my equilibrium," Milly admitted, glad to be able to speak openly to someone about her inner turmoil.

"Tell me more!" Sarah exclaimed with a smile and listened to Milly with rapt attention. "He sounds divine!" Sarah moaned with pleasure.

"I just get the feeling that I would have experienced real heartache if I'd been able to stay and see more of him. It wouldn't have had a happy ending," Milly said perceptively.

"But after such a short amount of time, your feelings are so strong for him; you have to admit that is terribly romantic!"

Milly laughed. "It has shown me just how shallow my feelings for Percy Connor were. I truly believe that Percy and I were not really in love. Seeing him should have affected me more than it has; I've been unmoved by the experience. Leaving Lord Grinstead behind is another matter. I physically feel as if I have left a part of me in London. It is irrelevant, though; we aren't likely to meet again unless I manage to get a position with a young girl who has yet to take part in the season in London, and that is highly unlikely."

"How are your enquiries going?"

"I've sent off two enquiries, but both were for elderly ladies. There aren't many advertisements for younger ladies; I expect family members are used in those instances. It's a pity because I would still like to enjoy a little bit of society from time to time, which is less likely with an elderly employer."

"If only your Earl had a younger sister that needed a chaperone, then you could fall in love and marry, once you'd found a good match for your charge, of course!" Sarah said with a wistful smile.

"I'd forgotten just what an incurable romantic you are! He's not my Earl, and he says that he's no family, so I doubt there is a sister waiting for my help."

"That is such a shame. I suppose he could have an illegitimate child somewhere who you could chaperone, but that would not aid the situation in regards to your romance. We don't need a jealous mistress in the background!"

"Sarah! If your husband heard you speaking in such a way, I doubt he would ever let you read a book again!" Milly laughed.

"It's the papers that are the worst," Sarah confessed. "You wouldn't believe the scandal that's reported in those pages. I have to wait until he's gone out before I touch them; he would be horrified if he realised I pour over them!"

"I'm not surprised!" Milly shook her head in amusement at her friend.

"I need some excitement in my life!" Sarah said with a laugh. Both friends knew she was perfectly happy with her lot.

"I could happily live without excitement," Milly responded with feeling. "Excitement usually brings trouble."

Chapter 7

Joshua was handed the crumpled sheet of paper. He grasped it as if he wanted to tear it into tiny pieces, but he could not. His image stared back at him as he glowered at the drawing. The two others in the room watched with interest at Joshua's reaction.

"Where did you get this?" he growled at the young man.

"It was in the pocket of one of them nosey-beaks," the young man responded, hoping that his find would bring him a reward. Roaming the streets, trying to make use of an opportunity had kept him alive so far, and he was always looking for the next chance.

"Nosey-beaks?"

"Those 'cise men."

"If the excise men have a picture of you, they're definitely still out to get you; they're going to a lot of trouble," Mack said to his fellow criminal.

Joshua's mind raced. Life had been difficult since the foiled landing in Dorset. The goods that should have been brought ashore with the French saboteurs had been seized. No funds could be raised from selling goods that did not exist! The fact that a number of his acquaintances had either been hanged or transported meant that many of the older channels of smuggling and criminal activity had been broken. There had been a lot less activity over the past weeks, and Joshua had felt deprivation because of it.

Forced to flee the Dorset coastline without any belongings and only the money he had in his pocket had meant a long hard journey back to the capital. He had managed to obtain a bed, but had been living on his wits until finally things seemed to be returning to normal. Other people had taken the place of the ones he lost, many willing to risk the fate of those gone before them in order to make money.

Just as he thought there was going to be an improvement in his finances, he was faced with the problem that excise men and goodness knew who else were still actively looking for him. He looked at the skin-and-bone youth standing before him. He had been the same once upon a time, and he was determined he was not going to be forced to live like an animal again.

"It has the printer's name on the bottom of the page. He's proud of his work," Joshua sneered. "Find out who ordered these. Do that, and I'll see you right."

"Aw, mister, I ain't able to live off fresh air," the youth moaned and, instead of receiving the clip around the ear that he expected, he saw Joshua smile for the first time. It was not a pleasant sight to witness; the scar that ran the length of his cheek seemed to open as a grotesque mouth on the side of his face.

"Be off with you," Joshua responded, flicking the boy a coin. "That's all you're getting until I have some more to go on. The quicker you are, the better the reward."

The boy caught the money, bit it once and turned on his heel with a nod of acknowledgement. He disappeared into the night as quickly as he had appeared.

"How will finding out who did this help you?" Mack asked.

"It won't, but I'll make sure they pay for it," Joshua responded with determination. He thought he had escaped, but it would appear not. He moved his fingers along his collar, almost as if he could already feel the hangman's noose around his neck. No, he was not going to be led down that path without a fight.

*

Henry rubbed his hands over his face for the umpteenth time that morning. He sighed as his hands landed with a thud on his desk; he had no idea what was wrong with him, but he was out of sorts. Nothing caught his attention; nothing diverted him; all he wanted to do was hide from the world, and that was unknown for the usually sociable Henry.

He had been to visit an old mistress of his. Greeting her with a kiss he had been disappointed when opening his eyes, he had been faced with green eyes instead of the clear grey eyes that haunted his dreams. He had pushed the image to one side determined to forget her, but he had been sharp with the woman who had immediately sensed there was something wrong.

He had left her residence shortly afterwards, both of them wondering what had happened to Henry. It had cost him an expensive trinket, which he had sent around a day later to apologise for his unusual behaviour.

It was no use; he had found comfort in knowing she was close by in London; he had not felt the need to seek her out, but she had been there. Now, she was miles away and, for the first time in his life, he was longing to be in someone's company.

After hours sitting at his desk, he slammed his hands down on the green leather-bound blotting pad. This was no good; he had to do something, only he no longer had the urge to be out seeking the enemies of the state. He would visit his estate for a while; that was bound to block out everything and would reaffirm his determination to complete what he had set-out to do.

*

Joshua was dumbfounded. "The little bitch; I know who's behind this!" he spat as the words the boy had told him sank in.

"Why is a lord interested in you, Josh?" Mack asked, showing admiration that his acquaintance seemed to be more important than he had first thought.

"I dunno." Joshua had not realised that two members of the aristocracy were on the beach that night, but he did begin to wonder at the issue of the picture being linked to someone he had met while a house guest. He was sure Charles had something to do with it and was curious to find out if the young man had issued some sort of reward for Joshua. "I know the old maid who did this though, and she's going to pay for my face being all over London!"

He handed coins to the boy. "Number six Half Moon Street; find out where the family are and what's going on there. I need to find the spinster cousin."

*

Henry had been out for a walk. He chose to walk early these last few days, having his exercise before most of the *ton* arose from their beds. His face wore a grimace of a smile when he remembered how his peer Edmund would find the situation amusing; the sociable Henry avoiding the public.

He was to leave London on the morrow and, if his current mood was anything to go by, he would not be returning soon.

The thought of chasing Miss Holland and declaring his feelings had never entered his head; it was not the done thing as far as he was concerned. He had never lost his heart before, so he presumed this state of melancholic frustration would pass soon enough.

He handed his hat, cane and gloves to his butler and entered his study; pouring himself a large glass of wine, he took a large gulp. The rich red liquid slid down his throat, the moment of warmth providing some comfort to a man, who, these days, seemed to be permanently cold.

He sat down and started to write a missive to Edmund. He was sure to be returning to London while Henry was still absent, and he wanted to try to persuade Edmund to return to the work in which they had both been involved. Although it gave no pleasure to Henry, he was convinced that, once on his estate, his mind would be focused again; however, inevitably he would be surrounded by reminders that would cause him pain while at home. He took another large gulp of the drink; he had not returned home in quite a long time. He hoped to God the echoes of the only person he had truly loved would no longer haunt his every step. Everything at home reminded him of her and, at this moment, reminders were something that had to be faced. So, as much as he dreaded it, he had to go back to reaffirm his promise.

A knock on the door disturbed his thoughts, and he placed his glass down whilst acknowledging the sound. The butler entered the room and approached the table with a silver tray containing a card.

"M'lud, there is a *tradesman* wishing to speak to you," the emphasis on the word communicating fully what the butler thought of such a request. "He is most insistent, repeatedly saying that it is of utmost importance he speak to you. I have threatened to throw him out on his ear for his impertinence, but his demeanour has given me cause to consider that perhaps there is some truth in his words and he is not here just to waste your time."

Henry frowned. "Show him in." The card, clearly stated that it was the printer he had used to produce the leaflets who now wished to see him.

The butler left the room, and returned seconds later with the gentleman in question. He was no longer dressed in his large apron but wearing the reasonably good quality clothing of a moderately successful tradesman.

Henry nodded at his butler, and the door was closed behind the servant. "Your visit is a little unexpected, Mr Long."

"I'm sorry to interrupt you, my lord, but there's been some unwelcome visitors to my business these last few days," Mr Long responded.

Henry noticed for the first time a bandaged hand holding the hat that was being turned, the action revealing the discomfort of the man. "Please sit," Henry commanded. "Tell me what has happened."

Mr Long compiled with the instruction and immediately explained about the visit to his premises of a young boy. "At first I just thought he was up to no good, asking who had ordered the pictures to be printed, and he got a clip around the ear for his trouble and sent on his way," Mr Long said, wanting to reassure the Earl that he had not given the information freely.

"The next morning, when I was opening up–I do it on my own you see–the little blighter got me from behind and stuck a knife in my neck!" Mr Long, moved his collar slightly and revealed a small cut to his skin.

"Go on."

"Nearly gave me a seizure, I can tell you. Anyways, I'm no pushover, and I grabbed the knife; only the little blighter was too quick and pulled the blade from my hand." This time the bandaged hand was shown as evidence.

"Not too deep a cut, I hope," Henry responded.

"No, although it'll be a bugger to work with for a while," Mr Long acknowledged.

"Pray continue."

"Well, I admit that I was a little shocked at the speed of this young 'un, and the knife was pointed in my ribs as quick as you could say Jack Flash! I nearly came over a bit faint, I don't mind admitting; I thought my number was up!"

"Were you robbed?"

"Well, he did take my wallet, but that was after he'd found out what he wanted to know. He forced me to tell him exactly who had ordered the pictures I'd printed."

"Fine, so he knows I'm after him," Henry responded nonchalantly. It won't make much of a difference."

"That's not all, my lord," the shamefaced trader said.

"Go on."

"He wanted to know who had drawn the picture, and I refused at first and have a cut across my stomach as a result of my foolishness. See, I didn't want to involve the young lady, her being a proper sweet thing, and I thought you wouldn't want her mentioned."

Henry nodded slightly but maintained his silence. His mind was beginning to race, and an unwelcome heavy feeling developed in his stomach.

"He wouldn't let up, and I'll be forever ashamed to admit it, but I told him about her."

Henry paled. Joshua knew that Milly had provided the drawing that every authority figure in London, at his command, was now carrying about their person.

"Thank you for telling me. I appreciate your coming and informing me of what has happened. Let me pay you for your trouble."

"Why, my lord, I didn't come here for that!" Mr Long spluttered, but his eyes widened at the wad of notes Henry retrieved from the top drawer of his desk. There must have been thirty pounds at least.

"Take it with my thanks. I hope your wounds heal soon," Henry said brusquely. He needed to be alone to gather his thoughts.

Eventually, Henry sent out a missive to someone who he knew could find out what was going on. There was no longer any consideration about leaving London. Joshua Shambles knew who had commissioned the picture and who had drawn it. He would not have many congenial feelings towards either party, and Henry had to find out what Shambles was planning.

It was two long days before Henry received the visit he had been waiting for. "Come in," he said, welcoming the man into his home long after all the staff had retired to bed.

Handing the man a glass of port, Henry waited until the glass was drained. Dangerous work deserved at least one good glass of liquid before the questioning commenced.

"I hope you have news?"

"I wouldn't be here without it. Your Joshua is hopping mad that you and your young lady have spread his face all over London."

Henry ignored the remark about Milly being his and let the man continue.

"He's changed from when you've come across him in the past. He's more likely to be found in the shadows than trying to fleece someone in a gaming hell. The wound he's got on his face makes it more likely people will be repelled by him, and he's been looking for someone to blame. Your young Baron who inflicted the wound isn't around, but you and the young lady are and have added to his ill-feelings. He has his perfect face staring at him every time he sees that picture. It's up on the wall of his lodgings."

"How the hell has he not been picked up if he's in London?" Henry snapped.

"He's good. He's surrounded himself by loyal people. I doubt he will be seen anywhere that would risk him being seen by anyone linked to you. He's not stupid, although he might make a mistake because of this picture."

"How so?"

"He's raging mad and has had someone sniffing around the address of your young Baron, trying to find out where the young lady is. I hope you've got her somewhere safe. I wouldn't like to be in her shoes when he catches up with her."

Henry went cold. "Why her and not me? He could approach me anytime."

"You are a Lord, she is a spinster. No one makes a fuss if a nobody disappears, but they do if someone titled does. Joshua wants to avoid the hangman; if he goes after you he'd be guaranteed to swing, but the young lady needs teaching a lesson in his eyes. How far he will go in that...," the man shrugged, leaving the sentence hanging. Both recognised the truth in his words. If Milly were to disappear, what could her small family do? The reality was: very little. It would be presumed she had eloped with a lover, not that one of the most wanted men in London had caused her disappearance.

"Thank you, Mack," Henry said. "I need to take measures to stop him getting to her."

"She'd need a complete army to protect her; he's lost any conscience he might have had once upon a time. The young lad that found everything out for him won't forget his last visit to Joshua anytime soon," Mack responded remembering the beating he had been a witness to. Mack was a hard man; he had to be because of the work he was involved with, but even he had felt sympathy for the waif as he had been struck. "He was lucky to escape with his life. Luckily, I managed to see him afterwards, and he's now on his way out of the City, off to work on a big estate."

Mack left the house, leaving through the back garden, in order to fade into the shadows. Mack could have told Henry exactly where to find Joshua Shambles, but both men knew that Mack was working under cover for a reason and, thankfully, Henry did not realise who Mack was working with, or he would have tried to force Mack to reveal the location. Mack had a job to do, and the risk to Milly was not enough to threaten the success of that. Joshua was only a worker; they needed to find out who was really working against the King, and it was more than likely going to be someone high in either the peerage or the government. Mack was using Joshua to find out the others involved. If he turned him in, a vital communication channel would be lost, and Mack was not prepared to do that. He had done his good deed by warning Henry; now it was up to the Earl to protect himself and the girl. Mack had other tasks to worry about.

Henry was left in the house to pace across his study, cursing his involvement of an innocent. He had acted selfishly and the result could be that Milly paid for his actions.

Finally, he stopped pacing. There was nothing to decide; he had put her at risk; he had to ensure she was safe. He could not let another life be lost at the hands of Joshua Shambles.

Chapter 8

Milly walked each morning to the post office. It was for no other reason than to escape the house for a little while. She could easily have the letters delivered but chose to escape her mother for a short time each morning. It also meant she could meander through the town, enjoying the peace and freedom, very often calling in to see Sarah while on her travels.

It was always a pleasure to receive letters from Clara. She did not expect to hear from Charles; he had never been a prolific letter writer, but Clara wrote every few days, using the letters to express her wonder at the pleasure in being married and travelling with a man determined to enjoy every minute with his new wife. Milly was inordinately pleased for her cousin and her match; anyone who had seen the pair on their wedding day would have been convinced of a long-lasting bond.

There was another reason Milly preferred to be alone while perusing the letters, and that had to do with her own next appointment. It would be the first time she would be employed; being with family was not the same, especially when the family was as considerate as Charles and Clara had been. The adjustment to the situation she needed to deal with had to take place away from her mother's scrutiny. Mrs. Holland would not understand why Milly was saddened by the acceptance of a position.

This appointment would be a recognition that all possibility of marriage was lost. In her heart she knew the truth, but there had always been a fragment of hope that one day she would meet someone who would love her enough to marry her, whatever her age and lack of dowry.

She was not longing for Mr Connor; seeing him had convinced her that she had no feelings for her old beau and was actually questioning the depth and reality of her so-called love for him. She was not even allowing herself to pine after the man who filled her dreams and most of her waking thoughts; that was a dream too far, there was no worth in longing for something that had no grounding in reality.

So, after much soul searching, she had come to the conclusion that she was letting a piece of her heart long for an unrealistic ideal—something that was never going to happen. Her acceptance of her lot would make it far easier to absorb the information in the letter she had received that morning. Needing counsel she decided to visit Sarah.

Sarah listened to Milly before speaking. "So, you are determined to accept the position?" she asked when Milly had explained the letter that had caused her to be so perturbed.

"I haven't really any choice; I know that. It just seems so far away."

"Ireland *is* far away."

Milly smiled. "I know, but it sounds a very good position. Not an aged person but someone who is widowed early and wishes to have a companion."

"But what if she marries again?"

"Then I suppose I return home."

"I can't help feeling if you travelled all the way to Ireland, you would never return."

"I probably wouldn't in reality, and it's a thought that doesn't worry me; that's why I'm here, I suppose. Should I be concerned at making such a huge change? Apart from my brothers, Clara, Charles and yourself, there is little to keep me in England. Perhaps a new life will be the making of me!"

"Is that not enough people to make you stay closer?" Sarah asked sadly.

"It would be, but I have to face reality. I think I need to carve out a life for myself, if that makes sense?" Milly responded.

"Not really," Sarah admitted.

Milly laughed. "Sometimes it doesn't make sense to me either, but it feels as if I've been dependent on others all my life and, since father died, that dependency hasn't rested easy. It's harder to accept help when you are reliant on your extended family. At least this way I will be employed and making my own way in the world."

"We are all dependent on others, Milly. That wouldn't have changed if you'd married; you know that. Surely you would want to share in the joys of being an aunt when your brothers settle?"

"I would, but I don't want to become the maiden aunt who falls asleep at the side of the fire every evening constantly travelling around the country to stay with another unwilling relative. I don't wish to become that burden. If that happened I'm sure I would become as bitter as mother is, even if hers is caused through some of her own actions."

"Dreading family members staying might be the case in some families, but not in yours!"

"Not yet it isn't, but what of my nieces and nephews? Will they welcome me into their homes? It isn't fair to them or me. This way, I can earn my own money. I'm frugal, and one day I might return with enough to pay for a comfortable retirement. The pay is very good for this position, far more than any other that has been advertised."

"Which makes me all the more suspicious!" Sarah harrumphed. "You could be walking into all the horrors of a gothic novel for all you know!"

"I'm meeting the lady in question in two weeks!" Milly laughed. "She is currently in England visiting family and will be travelling through Guildford and has suggested meeting me there. If we both like each other, I will continue with her on her journey."

"I'm sure there would be positions equally as desirable in this country."

"None that I've found so far and, with Mother being so keen to see me gone, this is a good opportunity all round."

"I beg to differ! As your friend I cannot be happy that you are leaving and, although we'll still write, it won't be the same," Sarah said, reaching over and squeezing Milly's hand. "I'll miss you; it's been so good to see you again. I selfishly don't want you to go quite yet."

"And I will miss you," Milly responded, touched that her friend was so sad to see her leave the locality. "I wouldn't be doing this if I didn't feel it was for the best."

*

Milly walked slowly back to the Castle Street deep in thought. In some respects she was running away if she accepted the position, but she felt she had no choice. She was not overwhelmed by self-pity; she was positive the route she had taken was the ideal opportunity, in some ways putting her a little in control of her life and also widening her horizons. She determined to view it as an adventure. She had once complained to Lord Grinstead that she longed to travel, now was her chance.

She saw Mrs Connor walking towards her and groaned inwardly; why Mrs Connor felt the need to boast in Milly's presence she had no idea. Whether it was done through pure malice or from insecurity, Milly would probably never find out.

"Miss Holland! How pleasant to meet you; I was just on my way to visit your charming little house," Mrs Connor said, as always her smile never quite reaching her eyes. "I shall accompany you home."

Milly let the comment pass that Mrs Connor had been walking in the opposite direction to Castle Street and had to change direction to accompany Milly. They walked in silence for a few moments before Mrs Connor started the conversation once more.

"It must be pleasant to visit your mother after such an amount of time. I do hope you weren't avoiding us, Miss Holland!"

"Not in the slightest. My cousin needed a companion, and I was more than happy to oblige." Milly's tone was always a little wary around Mrs Connor.

"Things must seem to have stood still since you left us."

"Not at all; marriages have taken place, children have been born. Lives continue as they do everywhere."

"When do you think you will be leaving us once more? You seem to have been sending and receiving a large amount of correspondence." Mrs Connor looked very keen to know the answer to her question.

"I receive a number of letters from my cousin. She is enjoying writing about the sights she is seeing on her wedding trip."

"Oh, come Miss Holland! We are all friends here! Your cousin could not be such a prolific letter writer; I know on my own wedding trip I was too busy to write letters! You must tell me of what you intend!"

"If you don't mind I will keep my plans to myself at the moment; I would rather make my mother aware of any changes in my circumstances myself before broadcasting them to the town," Milly responded. One thing she did dislike about returning home was the fact that all her business was known. The postmistress was obviously keen to report the number of letters Milly had received.

Mrs Connor looked annoyed at Milly's response, but as they had reached Milly's home, she refrained from pressing further. As Milly moved to open the door, both ladies were aware of a carriage stopping beside them.

Milly turned, and her complexion flushed as she instantly recognised the coat of arms on the carriage door. The footman jumped down from the grand equipage, its shiny black body and four horses pulling it betraying the expensiveness of the barouche. The footman pulled the steps in place before opening the door and handing out the occupant of the carriage.

"Good afternoon, Miss Holland; it is a delight to see you looking so well on this fine day," came the silky smooth voice of Lord Grinstead.

Henry looked in amusement at Milly's flushed cheeks and shocked expression. He could not help himself, he enjoyed making a dramatic entrance, and he had achieved his aim with the reaction he was causing. He congratulated himself on looking his best; even if he was there for a specific purpose, it had not detracted from the fact that he had chosen his clothes that morning to enhance his colouring and figure; clothing that hugged his body, emphasising the muscles, always had the greatest impact.

Milly also looked well. He was loathe to admit how much he had missed seeing her, but for now any nonsensical thoughts were pushed to one side once he had admired her for a few moments. He was here to do the job of keeping her safe; he had convinced himself of that as the only reason he had travelled all this way and, as always, he was determined to do that job well.

"Lord Grinstead!" Milly responded, eventually her brain able to work once more and curtseying to Henry's bow. "I didn't expect to see you in Farnham." She did not like the fact that Mrs Connor was seeing her surprise and confusion, but it could not be helped.

"I decided I needed a trip out of London and remembered I'd not visited this quaint little town for some time. I am staying at the Hog's Back Inn for a few days." Henry smiled at Milly. He was aware they were being watched with interest by the lady accompanying Milly and turned his attention on her. She was not as pleasing on the eye as Milly, her rouged cheeks and many curls giving her the appearance of an overly made-up doll in his eyes, but as always he turned on the Grinstead charm. "And who is this delightful creature accompanying you?"

Milly recollected herself. "This is Mrs Connor. Mrs Connor, please let me introduce the Earl of Grinstead to you. Mrs Connor lives in what was my parent's home just on the outside of town, my lord. You will have passed it on your journey in."

Mrs Connor curtseyed deeply. "My lord, it is a pleasure to welcome you to our humble town."

"Thank you Mrs Connor, I'm delighted to be here." For once Henry was speaking the truth. Panic and worry for Milly's safety had driven him to venture here but, for the moment, he could put that to one side; she was here, safe and looking delightful.

"My lord, we were just about to enter and order some refreshments. Would you care to join us?" Milly asked, not sure whether her mother would be delighted at having a peer under her roof or cross that she would be obliged to use her finest tea.

"That would be very pleasant, if it isn't too much trouble and would give me the opportunity to distribute the gifts I have brought with me," Henry said, turning back to the footman who retrieved parcels out of the carriage.

Milly was surprised at his words but led the way into the house. She turned to see Henry bending slightly, removing his stovepipe before he attempted entry and smiled at the sight. He filled the doorway, and the hallway seemed smaller than usual with his bulk crammed into it.

The maid took their outer garments, and Milly led the way into the small drawing room. Mrs Holland was taken by surprise but her welcome was everything Milly hoped for. Before too long the small group was seated, enjoying tea and biscuits.

Henry put down his cup and saucer and reached for the parcels that had been placed next to him on the sofa. It amused him that Mrs Connor seemed more intrigued about their contents than the actual recipients of the presents.

"Mrs Holland, I hope you will accept these few items. Your daughter always spoke highly of you when we were in the same company in London and at your nephew's home in Dorset, and I feel as if I already know you," Henry said with a flourish.

Milly raised her eyebrows at him in amusement. She could not remember mentioning her mother, apart from when she explained about their change in accommodation, which had obviously given him much information.

Henry returned her look with one of mock innocence before handing Mrs Holland a large tea caddy, full of the finest green tea. This was then surpassed with the box of chocolates that he gave her, followed closely by a box of delights such as butter, sugar, biscuits and oranges that he explained he had obtained from his own orangery. The gifts were finished off by the giving of a fine silk shawl, which made Mrs Holland quite delighted with her guest.

Henry then turned to Milly. "Miss Holland, I couldn't resist bringing this for you." He handed Milly a heavy parcel, which when opened, contained books of blank paper, watercolour paints and pencils.

Milly flushed with pleasure. Paper was so expensive, she had resigned herself to drawing very little over the coming years; Charles had indulged her by keeping her supplied with paper while she stayed with him; he always explained it away by saying she had saved him a fortune by painting his portrait. Now though, she would have enough paper to draw to her heart's content.

"Thank you, my lord," she whispered, genuinely touched. "You have been too kind."

"Not at all. You have real talent; I didn't want you getting lazy and not using it," Henry responded softly. He had surprised himself at how much pleasure had flooded his body at the sight of her delight; anyone would have thought he had given her jewels.

"How long do you stay, my lord?" Mrs Connor asked, having been quiet throughout the exchange of gifts, but fully aware of exactly what had been given; that information would be retold when she left the house.

"I'm not quite sure as yet. I'm waiting for some communication from a friend before I continue, so my plans are flexible at the moment," Henry lied. He would stay until he was sure that Milly was safe; beyond that he had not considered.

"I hope you will be around to enjoy a little party we are having on Thursday," Mrs Connor gushed. "It is only a small affair, but I believe the local families enjoy themselves at my home."

"I would be delighted," Henry responded, with a winning smile. "And if you are not already taken, I would like to secure the first two dances with you, Miss Holland."

The look of disappointment on Mrs Connor's face was almost comical, but Henry schooled his features, turning to Milly waiting for her response.

"I am not already engaged, my lord."

"Good, that is settled then! And I warn you ladies, I shall be looking to the married ladies for a dance or two; there'll be no hiding with the chaperones from me!" Henry said, making Mrs Holland blush with his smile.

"As I'm the same age as Miss Holland, I'm not seen as quite beyond my dancing days just yet, my lord," Mrs Connor said, a trifle indignant. She stood, preparing to leave. "I shall see you all on the morrow, I am sure. Good day to you all."

Mrs Holland walked Mrs Connor to the door, enjoying seeing the annoyance on the woman's face at being considered an old married woman. Mrs Holland had been made to feel lowly since her folly had been made so public, and she was not about to let an opportunity pass by for feeling at least on an equal footing with Mrs Connor.

"My lord, that was a wicked thing to do!" Milly whispered, but her voice held a laugh.

"I couldn't resist," Henry responded. "Sometimes people should really be aware of their every expression; they give so much away, and it seems a shame not to enjoy their foolishness. Surely you can allow me some amusement, Miss Holland?"

"I suppose this once I can allow it, especially as she will now be all over town, telling everyone about our unexpected visitor and his extravagant gifts; yes, I can definitely allow a little leeway," Milly acknowledged. "But be careful, she is one of the top members of our society."

"I won't upset her enough that she would take out her spite on you," Henry responded with feeling. She had been upset and put at risk too much already because of his actions.

"She won't have much time to take anything out on me, but I worry about her cutting tongue being used against Mother. If all goes to plan, I shall be leaving in two weeks."

"Leaving? Why on earth would you be leaving? Are you returning to your cousin?" Henry asked in surprise.

"I'm travelling to Ireland to be a lady's companion," Milly said. It was more for her own sanity that she was uttering the words. Seeing him had sent her heart in a number of flights of fancy; a flicker of hope had ignited that he might have visited to see her. Saying the words out loud reminded her that they were completely different people with no real possibility of a permanent connection.

In her own turmoil, she failed to notice the paling of Henry's face.

Henry had felt his stomach lurch at the thought of her travelling overseas and out of his life forever. He was torn between anger that she would consider what was, in his eyes, such a foolish plan and the fact that he would never see her sparkling grey eyes again.

"Ireland, Miss Holland? You can't go to Ireland!" Henry spluttered, surprising both Milly and himself at the force of his words. "I'll never see you again!"

Chapter 9

Mrs Holland returned to the drawing room very pleased that the afternoon had turned out so well. It was a shame that Lord Grinstead looked a little out of sorts and soon made his excuses and left, although he had visited for far longer than was usual.

"I do hope you have a suitable gown for the ball. I expect Lord Grinstead is used to seeing only the finest of materials," Mrs Holland fretted when their guest had gone.

"As he's danced with me previously, I'm sure my attire will be acceptable," Milly responded a little sharply. She did not wish to give her mother false hope that his visit was anything other than a coincidence, and it was becoming wearing that Milly was constantly a disappointment to her parent. She would not normally snap at anyone, in fact, but the way Henry had responded to her news had confused her even more.

The following morning Milly came out of the post office, having sent off a letter confirming her attendance at the planned meeting in Guildford when her breath caught in her throat. Riding down the road towards her was Henry on a large chestnut coloured horse, his brown frockcoat almost blending into the skin of the horse where it touched. The picture was perfect; rider and animal in harmony with each other. It was a sight that Milly would love to reproduce on paper.

She swallowed, her mouth going suddenly dry as Henry dismounted. They bowed and curtseyed, and Henry fell into step beside her, leading the horse with his left hand and offering his right arm to Milly.

"May I accompany you, Miss Holland?"

"I was only returning home, but you are welcome to join me," Milly responded, placing her hand on his offered arm. It was good to be in contact with his body even though it was only his arm. Even that seemed strong and sure, something she noticed about Henry: he was always so strong, it was reassuring. Then she shook herself at her own foolish thoughts– when had this change taken place within her? Not so very long ago she was cursing him to the devil. She silently cursed her fickleness and inconsistency.

"Is there a longer way to walk? It would be pleasant to stay outdoors where we can talk privately." Henry had to impart the news that she was potentially at some risk, although he was not convinced Joshua would seek her out so far from London.

"That sounds ominous."

"Before we start, I'd like to ask you why on earth you are going to Ireland," Henry asked, voicing the words that had been bothering him since he had left her home the previous afternoon.

"It's not yet decided, but there is a companion's position available with a young widow. It means I won't have to become the servant of an elderly lady, of which I could not be enthusiastic," Milly responded honestly.

"I'm surprised you wish to be anyone's companion. Why not stay at home?"

"I'm not in the fortunate position of having an independent income, my lord," Milly responded, her tone a little defensive.

"It's an impertinent question, I realise that, Miss Holland, but did your father not leave you any funds?" Henry asked, his tone gentle.

Milly sighed; she hated revealing her straitened circumstances, but he was no fool and had probably guessed much of her situation. "My father left nothing but debt. If it wasn't for Charles' kind support, we would be in a far worse position than we are now. He pays for my mother's home, my two brothers' schooling and has kept me for the last four years. No, there were no funds to provide a security blanket at Father's demise."

"It must have been hard moving out of your family home."

"It was, and it was made worse at the time because of other circumstances which are irrelevant today. So, you see, my lord, I need to earn my keep, and this is a perfect solution."

"What is your mother's opinion on the matter?"

"My mother isn't yet aware of my application but has encouraged me to obtain a position as soon as possible. As she points out regularly, she can't afford to keep me." Milly did not use the words to instigate sympathy, but she saw a tensing of Henry's face. "It is a fact of life that single women are a burden, my lord. Do not think I am wallowing in self-pity, for I am not."

"I think I would be in your position," Henry responded honestly.

"In that case, it's a good thing that our positions are different," Milly responded with a smile.

"But Ireland? Why Ireland?" Henry asked.

Before Milly had the opportunity to respond, she saw Sarah at a distance and started to smile. Henry noticed the smile and looked at the woman approaching them. "What's amusing you so much, Miss Holland?"

"The fact that I'm going to be providing gossip for my very good friend," Milly responded in merriment just as Sarah reached them. She watched Sarah assessing Henry, immediately realising who he was and was amused at the speculative look in her friend's eye.

Milly performed the introductions and, after Sarah had curtseyed, she smiled at Henry. "Ah, so you are the gentleman that Mrs Connor says comes bearing gifts when he visits, my lord. Feel free to visit me anytime and, in fact if you wish to take away a gift, I have many children you could choose from. I'm sure my husband would not notice if one or two went missing."

Henry laughed at Sarah's words. "I thought all ladies doted on their children, Mrs Hastings?"

"I do, I'd just prefer sometimes to dote on them at a distance!"

"Do not listen to her; her house is the most welcoming in the town," Milly interjected.

"You would make me out a liar in front of his lordship, Milly. Now, you know the only way I can prove my words to be true is by showing him exactly what I mean. If you would both like to, please come and take tea with me. I don't live very far from here, my lord."

"Miss Holland?" Henry asked, needing to speak to Milly further, but wanting to enjoy his time with her as well and not wishing to pass up an opportunity of seeing her at her most relaxed.

"I usually call in on my way home, so as long as we aren't keeping you from anything important, I'm happy to visit," Milly responded.

"I'm a tourist here, Miss Holland, so lead on, my time is yours!" Henry responded gallantly.

The threesome walked to Sarah's town house, and Henry handed his horse to a male member of staff. There was a small stable at the rear of the house, which was perfect to provide food and cover whilst Henry was socialising.

Henry smiled as he watched the two ladies. He had never stepped foot into a house like Mrs Hastings' before. The children were almost allowed free run of the house and had all run into the hallway to say their hellos when the group arrived.

Henry smiled down at the high-speed bundles flinging themselves at Milly and Sarah. They were a little more restrained with him, but only just. He looked down at the grinning child, just out of leading strings who was attached to his leg for support. The child seemed unconcerned at the unresponsive Henry.

A thought struck Henry; not so very long ago he would probably have shaken off the child in disgust that he might dirty his breeches or his boots, but looking from the child to Milly while wearing an expression of bemusement, he started to laugh. Something had happened to the great Henry, Earl of Grinstead, but he pushed the thought to one side, enjoying the fun and noise.

Eventually, they had extracted themselves from the children, who soon ascended the stairs and disappeared from sight. Noise could still be heard from the children's play, but it was dulled by the separation of two floors. Sarah led the way into a comfortable drawing room and settled her guests while refreshments were brought in. She poured tea and handed the cups around before settling herself onto an overstuffed chair.

"You said that you are a tourist, my lord. What sights are you hoping to see?" Sarah asked the moment she was happy that her guests had everything they needed.

"I was hoping to secure a guide who would show me the delights of the area," Henry said, with a pointed look at Milly.

Milly flushed slightly, knowing that Sarah would be enjoying her discomfort, as only a close friend could. "I'm sure I could spend some time showing you the local areas, although I'm sure you've mentioned that you've visited before," Milly responded a little tartly as she could see he was enjoying her discomfort.

"But never with such a willing guide! It's always best to be escorted by someone who knows the area so well and is such good company," Henry responded teasingly.

Sarah and Henry both laughed at Milly's harrumph.

*

Henry insisted on walking Milly home after their visit and asked again if they could walk somewhere a little private. Milly led the way into a small wooded copse that skirted the edge of the village.

"We can see anyone approaching, although I would rather not spend too long in here. I don't like giving the gossips too much pleasure," Milly said, pausing at a fallen tree trunk and carefully leaning against it.

"If there was another way of having this conversation I would choose it, but I feel your mother would not leave us alone for long enough."

"What is it that is so important?"

"I feel like the worse type of bounder, Miss Holland, I really do. You are in this situation because of me; and I can only apologise," Henry started.

Milly waited until Henry composed himself enough to tell her the full story. She could see he was agitated and was a little surprised at the emotion. When they had first met she would have sworn that he had no decent feelings.

Flowery words deserted Henry for the first time in his life. He had to be honest rather than behaving in his usual way. "Joshua Shambles knows who is behind the picture that is now circulating the underworld of London and, unsurprisingly, he isn't happy about the fact. I needed to let you know in order that you are on your guard and assure you that I'm here to protect you." Henry felt distinctly peculiar as he uttered the words. He did so want to protect her but was not convinced that it was as a result of the threat from Joshua. He began to question the effect Milly had on him; she moved him in ways he had never been affected before.

If Henry expected Milly to respond with fainting, remonstrations or curses, he was to be disappointed. She remained quiet for a few moments before meeting his gaze with her own clear one. "I appreciate your offer of protection and will avail of it. You have made a good case of your reasons for being here to the few people you've met. There should be no surprise if you visit here for two weeks and then continue on your travels. I shall also take more care, although I can't envisage anyone following me here but, hopefully, if a stranger appears, they will be soon seen. I'm sure no one will be distressed at your being in our society; we rarely have Earls visiting our parlours. We are both aware of your ability to convince people you are one thing when in reality you are another."

Henry thought he could detect a note of bitterness, but it was so soon disguised he was not completely sure. "I'm sorry you have to be inconvenienced because of your involvement with me."

"I shall be gone in two weeks, so it will be an inconvenience of short duration. Shall we recommence our walk?"

Milly led the way out of the copse more annoyed with herself than she was with Henry. She had allowed her heart to rule her head, and now she felt the fool she was. He had followed her to Farnham not because she attracted him but out of obligation and a sense of duty. Well that had certainly put her in her place; and she would remember her foolishness until she could escape to Ireland and start a new life where no one knew of her foolish heart.

They walked in silence back to Castle Street; Milly was contemplating the importance of speaking to Sarah. They had both read too much into Henry's visit.

Henry was trying to console himself over the fact that his actions had driven a wedge between them once more. It was clear from her silence that she wished him a hundred miles away; it was a pity that the thought depressed him.

Selfishly, he could take some enjoyment of the need to spend the next two weeks with her, but the fact that she would be leaving at the end of them to travel to another country made him long to stop her somehow. He silently cursed himself; he was a complete cad; she was in danger and had the perfect escape plan, and he wanted to prevent her leaving for his own selfish reasons.

He deserved to be flogged for being so wrapped up in his own needs.

Chapter 10

Milly should have been able to enjoy the following few days. She had an escort everywhere she went. If she left the house, he would appear. If she visited someone, he would not be far behind. If she stayed at home, he would visit.

It was driving her to distraction.

How cruel to have so much attention from the man she dreamt of every night and thought about from the moment she awakened; yet he was being so attentive out of obligation.

She had told Sarah the real reason Henry was staying in the area. She was sure of her friend's confidence in anything she had to say.

"He should have considered the risk before asking you to provide the drawing!" Sarah had exclaimed.

"I suppose his motivation was more about the country's security rather than the implications to me," Milly responded realistically.

"He should have an army of men around you day and night."

"That would certainly put a strain on mother's resources," Milly said with a smile at the lecture she had received only that morning from her mother.

"Well, at least he will be a good dancing partner for tonight's ball. I do wish Mrs Connor wouldn't try to Lord it over the town quite so much. We know she lives in one of the largest houses in the area, and yet she feels the need to remind us regularly just how important she is," Sarah said with a sigh. "I've got more important things to concern myself with than her inflated self-importance."

Milly smiled at the slight bulge in Sarah's dress. It would not be too long before Sarah was confined to more sedate pastimes once she could no longer disguise the impending birth.

*

Milly prepared for the ball with care. Her hair was twisted into the tightest curls then fluffed to create a soft framing of her face. She wore a little black soot mixed with a drop of oil on her eyelashes, she applied the mixture and then took a corner of a cloth and removed the excess. The result was a darkening of the eyelashes that looked natural and enhanced the grey of her eyes. She had practised the procedure with Sarah since returning; Sarah was always at the forefront of the latest trends even though she did not frequent fashionable London. She claimed to be determined to avoid becoming a rustic and spent a considerable amount of money on magazines and fashion plates, receiving them far earlier than many of her contemporaries.

Milly then applied Rigge's Liquid Bloom to her lips, a present from Clara. It gave her naturally rosy lips a transparent gloss, making them look fuller and drawing the eye to them.

Her dress was of a warm peach silk, a present from Charles. A matching peach overlay of fine organza was speckled with tiny cream flowers. The edges of the neckline, sleeves and hem were trimmed with deeper peach satin ribbon. She finished her outfit with cream satin gloves and a pearl necklace and ear rings. The jewels were paste, but it did not matter or detract from the overall effect.

Milly stood in front of her cheval mirror, running her hands down the length of her dress. For once she felt every inch the woman she could have been if circumstances had been different.

Not one for regrets she smiled at her reflection; picking up the cream silk shawl she wrapped it around her shoulders. She did not need her cloak tonight; Henry had insisted on escorting the mother and daughter in his carriage, promising hot bricks, rugs and warm drinks to help them on their short journey.

Henry felt his mouth go dry as he waited with Mrs Holland in the hallway of her house and watched Milly walk down the stairs. He had noticed that she was pretty when he had seen her in London, nothing compared to the diamonds of the season of course, but pretty and elegant in the way she held herself.

When they had been in Dorset, she had seemed to come alive a little. Whether it was because she had spent so much time out of doors, or if she was more comfortable away from the more formal role of being a companion, he had no idea, but she had certainly improved in looks. He had been moved enough to kiss her, although that had not been purely because of attraction, he acknowledged, which was to his everlasting shame.

Now though, as she walked confidently downstairs, she seemed to glow with good health and looks. The colour of her gown suited her perfectly, making her skin look warm, the material moving with a swish around her tall, slender figure. Her eyes seemed to draw him to her, as always looking at him as if she could see into his soul. Finally his eyes rested on her lips; they looked moist as if she had just licked them in readiness for being kissed and, once again, he had to swallow and try to focus so his body would move, ushering them out into the night. She would be his for the first two dances, and it was going to be hard to stop himself from touching her inappropriately.

Milly smiled at Henry, as he handed the two ladies into the carriage. He fussed over Mrs Holland, afraid of losing what little control he had over his faculties if he had to fuss over Milly. Thankfully, Milly was more than capable of tending to her own needs.

They set-off, letting Mrs Holland lead the conversation until they turned into the drive of the Connor's house.

"It will always grieve me to be a visitor in my own house!" Mrs Holland said, her mood unable to stay buoyant for long.

"Mother, we are here to enjoy ourselves; let us not go over the past now," came the plea from the long suffering daughter.

"It could so easily have remained in the family!"

"Mother!" Milly said in a warning tone.

Henry noticed the exchange and, even in the darkened carriage, could tell that Milly's cheeks had flushed in mortification. Not one to miss any signs, he was immediately alert that there was a part of the family history that had been omitted when Milly had told him their story. He determined to find out more.

*

Mrs Connor had put on as grand a ball as was humanly possible. As she had already informed the Hollands, no expense had been spared. The scent of the flowers that seemed to be tumbling out of every vase, jug and ledge almost overwhelmed the senses of the arriving guests. Garlands had been fixed to both banisters of the staircase, the amount of foliage wrapping around the newel hiding the wooden structure completely.

Candles blazed out of every sconce, chandelier and candelabrum, leading the way into the large double length drawing room, which was normally separated by large wooden doors for daytime use. A pianoforte in the corner was already being played by a hired musician, and a singer was singing an Italian melody, to which most guests were only giving passing notice, being more intent on speaking to friends and acquaintances.

Mrs Holland separated from Henry and Milly, seeing some of the elder members of the town who would be willing to give her a sympathetic ear. Milly continued through the drawing room, which opened onto the ballroom, a large room running across the side of the house.

There were fewer flowers in this room, but it was still decorated extravagantly. A three-piece orchestra were seated at the far end of the ballroom, playing quietly before the dancing started. Milly smiled when she saw Sarah and her husband Peter, making their way through the crush to them.

"I'm sure there aren't this many families normally in town at this time of year," Sarah said, looking flushed and using her fan vigorously.

"No one wants to miss this event," Peter said good-humouredly after the introductions with Henry had been made.

"It's seems an event that is determined to make a statement," Henry said observing the signs of wealth from the number of footmen serving drinks to guests and the number of plates of food that could be seen already laid out in the dining room. Far more food would be distributed before the end of the evening; the platters already available were only for those who could not wait for the main dishes to be served. The morning room and the breakfast room were reserved for those who wished to play cards.

"It is the highlight of the year. Apparently!" Sarah said mischievously.

"Which you wouldn't miss for the world," Peter responded.

"Unfortunately this year I won't be dancing, unlike Milly who is sure to be the belle of the ball."

"Mrs Connor rightly holds that title," Milly said, looking warningly at her friend.

"I think tonight Mr Connor might be experiencing a pang that probably feels a lot like regret and with that I shall go and sit with the older ladies; thankfully I will be rejoining the dancers next year," Sarah said airily before leading her husband to the edges of the ballroom where they were soon surrounded by friends.

"Your friend is a force to be reckoned with," Henry said pleasantly.

"I thought marriage and motherhood would have mellowed her, but it appears to have made her even more outrageous," Milly admitted.

"Shall we?" Henry asked as the orchestra prepared to start the first dance.

"I'd be delighted," Milly responded honestly. How could she not welcome the opportunity of dancing with the most eligible man in the room? His dark frock coat, cream breeches and shining boots, all combined to make him stand out above everyone else. His figure filled his clothing, making the material appear to be straining against the muscular body. Yes, Milly was going to enjoy the next hour.

Milly was surprised when they were joined by Mrs Connor. "My lord, you must join us at the top of the set," Mrs Connor said, almost rounding them up as she chivvied them up the line of people already taking their places. "No one could ever say I don't know how to give rank it's precedence." She hurried them along, her dress edged in some feather-like material which made her slightly rounded figure look decidedly rotund.

Milly would have rather started the set lower down as she was now in a set of four with two people she would have preferred to avoid. Some of the pleasure had been taken out of the next hour, but she could not help returning the smile that Henry was giving her.

They started to move through the dance, and Henry saw that Milly was uncomfortable every time she had to make contact with Mr Connor. It was very interesting. There was obviously some history, and it did not need a genius to work out why Mrs Holland berated her daughter about no longer living in the home. Mrs Holland had clearly wanted Milly to marry Mr Connor.

Henry felt the smile on his face slip as he thought that Mr Connor might be the person who had shared Milly's first kisses. He frowned darkly as the gentleman passed him in the set, looking at Henry in surprise before a glance at Milly caused him to flush. Henry glowered at the man; he had obviously guessed correctly.

The remainder of the dance passed in discomfort for three of the set of four. Only Mrs Connor seemed oblivious to the undercurrent that was making the two dances pass inordinately slowly. Finally, when the second dance came to an end, Henry bowed to Milly and the Connors before taking Milly's hand and placing it firmly on his arm in an act of possession. He walked through the milling crowds until they reached the edge of the ballroom.

"My lord?" Milly asked a little puzzled at the change in behaviour. She had been so wrapped up in her own discomfort she had failed to notice the change in Henry until the end of the second dance. True, there had been little conversation during the dance, but she had presumed that was on account of herself not wishing to enter into any chatter; every word she could have uttered would have been overheard by the Connors, and she wanted to avoid that at all costs.

"You've kissed that man!" Henry hissed at her; although he was angry, jealous and nettled, all rolled into one confusing swirl of emotions, he kept his voice low. He was not about to expose her to anyone else's censure, apart from his own of course.

Milly could not prevent the flush spreading across her cheeks, but she faced Henry her head held high. "I did." His angry reaction to the knowledge was baffling to say the least, but she was not going to deny something she had done in the flush of youth when she had been engaged and believed herself to be in love. Kissing the man she should have spent the rest of her days with had not been wrong then and she was not going to feel shame for it now.

Henry would swear afterwards that someone had kicked him forcefully in the stomach, the pain was so intense. Some indication of the pain he felt flashed across his face before he schooled his features into a more appropriate one. "And can I ask when these kisses occurred and why you would kiss a man who is now married to another?"

The censure and condemnation in Henry's voice brought tears to Milly's eyes. Angrily blinking them away, she wondered what it was about Henry that turned her into a watering pot. She rarely cried and yet, here she was, the second time in not too many weeks wanting to cry over the opinion that Henry had of her. Was it bitter regret that he could not see her in a different light? Probably, she mused, trying desperately to get herself back under control.

Milly thrashed about in her mind for how best to respond. She could not storm away from Henry; a scene was the last thing she wanted to cause. Eventually, she stood straight and looked Henry directly in the eyes. "You are here to protect me from the perceived threat of Joshua Shambles. Keep your impertinent questions to yourself, my lord; I am under no obligation to explain my actions now or in the past to you or anyone else. Please excuse me."

Milly turned and left Henry at the side of the ballroom. The next dance was underway; no one noticed Henry balling and releasing his fists as he tried to calm himself. He wanted to pummel Mr Connor into at least the next century, but he could not. He had no right to feel so insanely jealous, but his reasoning did not ease the intense feeling he was suffering from. Outwardly, the only indication of his turmoil was a muscle twitching in his cheek.

He was eventually disturbed by the approach of Sarah. "Shall we seek some refreshment, my lord? This evening is proving to be uncommonly hot," she said, still wafting the ever present fan.

Henry nodded slightly and followed the woman through the ballroom and into the dining room. They were both handed a glass of wine, and Sarah sat in an alcove, indicating that Henry should join her. Insipid conversation was the least attractive prospect at the moment, but Henry complied with Sarah's request with only the smallest of sighs. He was amused to think that his friend Edmund would be laughing loudly at Henry's discomfort; Henry had always been the social butterfly of the two of them, making them both perfect to act as spies for the state. Henry was welcome in the highest households, his charm and wit making him a popular guest, whereas Edmund had been welcomed in the less salubrious establishments until he had met his new wife.

"Now then, my lord, I have an inclination that you are not happy with my dear friend," Sarah started. Milly had only needed to say the fewest of words before Sarah had grasped the situation and, although Milly had sought an escape from Henry into the drawing room, Sarah had sought out the peer.

"In truth I don't know what I am, Mrs Hastings," Henry answered honestly, for the first time voicing his confusion.

Sarah hid a smile; it seemed very likely that Milly had ensnared the eligible Earl after all. "Milly doesn't like speaking about that time."

They spoke quietly to each other, but the people visiting the room for food and drink were transient enough to not be able to overhear their conversation.

"I'm not surprised."

"And yet you don't know the story," Sarah responded, looking at Henry with an expression of annoyance and disappointment. "You have condemned my friend without knowing what happened and what she was put through."

"I don't understand."

"Of course you don't. Most people in this town don't either. It's little wonder she stayed away for over four years. There was a time when I thought she would never return," Sarah said sadly.

Henry's anger and jealously started to be replaced with feelings of dread. "What happened?"

"Those, my lord, are the first reasonable words you have uttered so far! Seeking the truth instead of presuming the worst as so many do. There is hope for you yet."

Henry raised his eyebrows but refrained from speaking.

"Milly and Mr Connor were engaged to be married." Sarah noticed with reassurance the sharp intake of breath but did not react or comment on it. "He's always been a little full of his own self-importance in my eyes, but he romanced Milly until she was utterly smitten with him. We didn't know it then, but he was very motivated to achieve exactly what he wanted."

"Milly's father was in far too much debt, and it was catching up with him. In fact, before she left Milly confessed to wondering if he took that walk in the pouring rain purposely hoping to catch a chill. As you know, he did fall ill and died as a result. It was only hours after the death when the creditors started knocking on the door. News travels fast and people who are owed money make their claim quickly."

"Had the family no idea?" Henry asked.

"If the boys had been older, maybe they would've noticed, but with only Milly and Mrs Holland at home, so many debts could be hidden. I was with Milly when the first creditors knocked. She was grieving for her father whilst being faced with caller after caller. I will never forget the expression of hurt and bewilderment as Milly asked herself why she had not noticed or guessed that he was overspending. At that point she didn't blame her parents; now though, she has had time enough to realise that both her parents were foolhardy in the way they lived their lives. A shame it is their children who have suffered as a result."

"Connor?" Henry queried, knowing that there was no happy ending to the story.

"Milly's cousin, Charles, immediately came down to support the family and try to find out what could be done to help. They presumed that Milly would be taken care of since she was already engaged. Her dowry had been reasonable, but not huge and, although lost, it shouldn't have affected their overall lifestyle; Mr Connor had some funds. Unfortunately, for Milly there was a blow to occur none of us foresaw."

"She called off the engagement? Why would she do that?"

"Nothing so simple, my lord. Mr Connor, the man who had pursued her so diligently, quickly took stock of the situation and informed Milly that he could no longer marry her. It caused an uproar within the family, but he offered, professing to be a gentleman while he uttered the vile words that he would allow Milly to call off the wedding. That way she would save some of her reputation and would dampen a little of the gossip that was inevitable."

Henry felt sick. A girl who had no dowry and was reputed to have called off an eligible engagement would be the laughing stock of the town; although it would be better that than to know her beau had withdrawn his offer. Her reputation would be irreparably damaged whichever way she chose to act.

"Yes, I see you recognise the issue," Sarah said approvingly. "Milly refused to call the engagement off, saying that she had made the commitment and nothing had changed in her eyes. I think in some way she was trying to test him, which of course he failed spectacularly. So, the result of the horrible situation was he ended the engagement. There was no possibility of stopping the gossip, and oh, they were so shocked; nothing else was spoken of for weeks. You can only imagine what it was like, but to those who were close to Milly, it was horrendously cruel."

"The poor girl." For the first time in a long time Henry felt the anger he had experienced once before at the unjust way situations could so easily turn out. It bubbled beneath his reasonably calm surface, but anyone seeing his eyes would have stepped back at their fierceness.

"Yes, exactly. She kept her own personal integrity but became the talk of the town. That increased tenfold when, three weeks after the split, Mr Connor arrived in Farnham with his new, very wealthy wife, who we'd all known growing up. The family had moved away, the father going into business somewhere in Portsmouth and making a very large profit. It was a surprise that they returned to Farnham really; most don't want to broadcast to the people they socialise with that they have made their money through trade. Mrs Connor's parents wanted a large house for their newly married daughter and, of course, Mr Connor knew of the perfect one."

"He could have picked anywhere in the country," Henry ground out.

"Exactly. He lost a lot of goodwill by moving into this house. It was as if he was flaunting what he'd done in front of Milly when she'd done nothing wrong. Milly left the area with her cousin to join Clara as companion soon afterwards, and we haven't seen her for four long years."

"She shouldn't have hidden from everyone."

"I don't think she was hiding after the first few months had passed. You've seen Mrs Holland and can appreciate what a—let's just say what a character she is; I think Milly began to enjoy her time with her cousins," Sarah said trying to be diplomatic and failing.

Henry smiled. "Yes, Miss Holland has alluded to her mother's foibles."

"The pathetic thing is that, since Milly's return, both Mr and Mrs Connor seem to always need to make Milly feel uncomfortable in order to prove to themselves of their own happiness. I don't understand their motivation."

"I can understand the wife. She must know she was married purely for her money," Henry mused.

"Perhaps, but there is no need to take it out on my friend. It seems everything is done to make Milly fully aware of what she lost. It wouldn't be so bad, but Mrs Connor played with us all as children; since then she seems to have forgotten the loyalty that friends should share," Sarah said crossly.

"Milly has a good friend in you, Mrs Hastings."

"But I can only do so much, as can be seen by her intent on travelling to Ireland. We will never see her again, of that I'm sure. I wish there was a way of keeping her here, but also stopping her being the target of the Connors at the same time."

"If you would excuse me Mrs Hastings, I've a few things to mull over," Henry said suddenly, standing and making his bow to Sarah. Henry needed to clear his head of everything that was flying around inside, and a house holding a large ball was definitely not the place to do it.

He made his way through the throng and, after speaking to a footman, entered into the study. Closing the thick wooden door brought some peace from the noise of the evening. He needed time to process what he had been told. He would never have guessed that there was such a history between Milly and the Connors, but it did explain some of their behaviour towards her. He tried to push the feelings of anger and jealousy to one side. The man who had experienced her first tentative kisses had not deserved them.

One thought whirled around his mind, and each time it seemed to spiral into a tighter, more disturbing thought. She could still be in love with Mr Connor. He tried to push it away; she did not deserve his anger, but every time he allowed the thought to penetrate into his consciousness, he felt a rage that made him shake.

He needed to speak to her, so opening the door, he directed a footman to locate Milly and ask for her to see him. The large coin he gave the servant would ensure that the footman carried out the task discreetly.

Henry paced in front of the large desk that filled the room until the door opened slowly, revealing Milly. "My lord?" she asked curiously.

"Miss Holland, forgive me, but I need to speak to you," Henry said, crossing the room and gently pulling her over the threshold and closing the door behind them. No one of importance noticed her entrance as the hallway was busy with staff rather than guests, everyone in the midst of the evening's entertainment.

"At a ball?" Milly was intrigued but also aware that their behaviour was foolish at best.

"I've heard what happened between you and that beast Connor," Henry ground out. It had perhaps not been his finest idea to start the conversation when he was still so angry.

"Oh," came the dull response.

"Oh? Is that all you have to say on the subject?" Henry almost exploded, but he did not grasp the reason why.

"What else is there to say? I was rejected by the man I thought loved me, and now every time I see him or his wife, it's as if they are laughing at me. Would speaking of my confusion make the situation better? I think holding my counsel on the subject is far more preferable for everyone concerned. You never know;

they may tire of what they are doing, either intentionally or unintentionally; I haven't dwelled on it enough to decide which." Milly had responded more heatedly than she would have normally, but the evening had been a strain, one that had made her head pound with tension. To be faced with Henry making goodness knew what assumptions of the whole sorry episode had pushed her over the edge of restrained, civilised conversation.

"No it wouldn't make it better. How can you stand to see the man that you are without doubt still pining for lording it over your ancestral home?" Henry asked savagely. That was it he realised, the reason he was so angry. Apart from being angry because of her mistreatment, he was incensed at the fact she was still in love with Connor.

"Wait one moment! I'm still pining for him?" Milly asked in disbelief. "Why on earth would I long for someone who broke my heart and embarrassed me in front of everyone I had ever known? Have you completely lost your mind, my lord?"

"Yes, I think so."

Milly was surprised at the response but waited to see if there would be any further explanation. The whole evening had been an unmitigated disaster in her eyes, and she could not wait to return home.

"I'm sorry," Henry finally said. "I can't help it."

"Help what?"

"That I want to be the only one who kisses you," Henry said before enfolding Milly into his arms and kissing her every bit as urgently as he had the last time she had sent his emotions tumbling over each other.

Milly wrapped her arms around Henry's neck, fully responding to his kisses. They were, after all, what she had been dreaming of for weeks. This time was different though; this time he had said he wanted to kiss her; perhaps he felt something of the confusion she was suffering.

She sighed as he moaned her name, deepening his kiss. She had only experienced his touch once before, but she had missed it every day since. He would have to be the one to stop the kisses; Milly did not have the will to pull away.

They were both so engrossed that neither were aware that the door had opened until they were brought to their senses by the words. "My Good God! I don't believe I am seeing this!"

Mr Connor faced them with a furious expression, his anger aimed mainly at Milly. "Miss Holland! I feel you have gone too far in sullying our home with your wanton behaviour!"

Chapter 11

Milly tried to spring away from Henry but she was prevented by his arms holding her firmly but gently in place.

Henry turned to Mr Connor, standing like an indignant father in the doorway. "Sullying your home?" he said his voice still husky from the emotion of the kisses.

"Yes, I expect appropriately respectable behaviour from my guests, not this impropriety! Although I suppose I shouldn't be really surprised!" Mr Connor snapped, glaring at Milly.

"And yet you have aimed your censure at one of us, not both," Henry mused, making Mr Connor look uncomfortable. Henry smiled down at Milly, adoration in his eyes. "Explain to me how kissing the woman I am to marry is something we should apologise for? Did you never exchange kisses when you were betrothed? I'm more than certain you did. Which makes your words slightly hypocritical don't you think?"

Mr Connor looked between the pair; his face had flushed at Henry's words, his expression one of annoyance. "If you are betrothed, may I be the first to wish you happy. Your mother hasn't mentioned anything Milly."

Milly had stiffened in Henry's arms when he made the announcement, but at Mr Connor's words, she took a breath as if to speak. Henry swooped down and kissed her quickly but firmly, preventing any words being uttered. "We haven't announced it as yet. I'm the happiest of men because I've got the best of women to agree to be my wife. My darling is assured that I want her and no other. Everyone will be jealous, and rightly so, wouldn't you agree Connor?"

"Of course," Mr Connor said, but looked anything but happy at the words he was forced to utter out of politeness. "I shall leave you alone and look forward to your announcement when you make everyone aware of the happy occasion."

Henry smiled at the calling of his bluff. "We shall be through shortly. Close the door on your way out, Connor."

Mr Connor used more force than was necessary when he slammed the door behind him. Henry moved to kiss Milly once more, but she placed her hands flat against his chest and pushed away from him.

"Why on earth did you say that, of all things?" she asked in disbelief. Her whole body was shaking, and it was not as a result of the kisses.

"We were caught in a compromising position. I wasn't allowing him the upper hand after what he did to you."

"Laudable sentiments, my lord, but your actions are a little extreme, even for you." Milly did not know whether to laugh or cry at Henry's words.

"This is why I need to marry you; you constantly prevent me running ahead of myself. I find the thought reassuring that I'll always be able to rely on you to keep my over-inflated ego firmly in its place," Henry said with a smile. The words about a marriage had been uttered in the heat of the moment, but the more he thought about marrying her, the more the idea appealed to him.

Milly shook her head. "Impossible man!" Her legs had almost given way when he had stood up to Mr Connor and saved her from censure and ruin, but he would change his mind, of that she was sure. It had been a gallant gesture but not one she would take seriously. She had to be practical about it.

"Maybe so, but we need to make an announcement to your friends and family, or there will be repercussions. It is a perfect solution to everything; I'm surprised I didn't think of it earlier. Joshua Shambles wouldn't dare to approach you if you were Lady Grinstead. I like the sound of that," Henry smiled.

Milly shook her head; everything was running too fast; she had to take control. "Stop! Please!" she begged, her hands at each side of her face as if the action would stop the noise. "I'm not going to marry you. I refuse to have my heart broken when you decide that you've changed your mind."

"I wouldn't."

"What, you could promise me love, faithfulness and honesty? Being a traditional husband with no running around putting yourself in danger by spying for the King?"

"I could try," Henry said.

"And you wouldn't be bored within a week when you feel obliged to come to me every night instead of frequenting whatever clubs you belong too?"

"I don't think marriage means turning into a hermit!"

"No, it doesn't. It does mean considering another's needs, sometimes above your own. Are you really prepared to consider my needs for the rest of your days?" Milly asked reasonably.

"It surely isn't so bad?" Suddenly Henry was beginning to realise the reality of his words. Marriage meant no longer being able to do exactly as he wished. He had been carried away with the thought of being with Milly but, of course, there were the everyday monotonies to consider. That thought certainly put a dampener on his thoughts, but he tried to keep smiling.

Milly saw that the smile no longer reached his eyes, and her heart sank even though she had been expecting the response. "Trying isn't good enough. I need to be with someone who wants to be with me above all others. As I found out with Mr Connor, second best doesn't result in happy endings."

"Don't class me the same as that fortune hunter!" Henry spat.

"Both of you don't want me as a person, so in that respect you are similar; although I do concede that the circumstances are different; you are acting out of chivalry, for which I thank you. It isn't enough though is it? It would be a disaster," Milly said sadly.

"I want you," Henry said, moving across to Milly and cupping her face in his hands. He kissed her gently. "I do want you."

Milly pulled away. "Wanting isn't enough, as much as everyone will consider me a fool," she said quietly. She could so easily go along with what he said and marry the man she loved, but she had to be realistic. He would hurt her a thousand times more than Mr Connor had, and she was not sure she would survive that level of misery.

"We'll have to announce our engagement, or there will be consequences for you." Henry realised that he had gone too far and was not going to upset her further. He had never caused anyone to look at him the way Milly was now, and inside it was tearing him apart. It was as if he could see her heart breaking through the anguish in her eyes, and he was stirred deeply, which seemed to be occurring more and more with Milly. He just wanted to make things better for her and yet he had caused this.

"As I leave in two weeks, I suppose it won't really matter. We shall have to make some reason why we are marrying away from Farnham and, if you leave at the same time as I, no one will be any wiser." Milly was as practical as ever.

"You wouldn't be able to return home."

"I probably wouldn't have done anyway. I'd accepted that this would quite possibly be my last visit."

Henry wrapped Milly in his arms, tucking her head under his chin. It was an embrace of true feeling. Milly enclosed his waist with her arms and rested her cheek on his chest. The unprompted act of kindness had brought a tear to her eye, and she did not wish to be exposed. She closed her eyes, listening to the steady, strong heartbeat of the man she loved.

Eventually, Henry pulled away slightly. "Come, let's get this over with. At least I will be engaged to you for two weeks, even if it is a sham."

*

Mrs Connor had seemed out of sorts that the highlight of her social year had to be shared with Milly and Henry's unexpected announcement. She, along with her husband, had played the perfect hosts, but both had worn strained expressions once the announcement of the betrothal had been made.

Sarah and Mrs Holland had been happy beyond words, but Milly had whispered a few words that had caused Sarah to frown then nod with some comprehension. Of all people Milly could not lie to her friend.

After a sleepless night, Milly had breakfasted as best she could and then walked directly to Sarah's home. She did not wish to visit the post office or any other public venue; the strain of maintaining the pretext would be too much after so little sleep.

Sarah fussed with tea while watching her friend. "I would've expected a newly engaged friend, especially to someone as handsome and charming as Lord Grinstead, to be far happier than you are, my dear. What did you mean when you said you'd explain everything?"

Milly told Sarah the sorry tale and, after she had stopped speaking, Sarah sighed. "I know you hadn't set out for any of this to happen, but it would solve everything in a way that would be better for you. You would have his protection and his title and money; you wouldn't need to work ever again. Is it not worth considering going through with the marriage?"

Milly wondered how much stronger Sarah would argue for the match if she knew just how serious Henry was treating the risk from Joshua. Milly had played the situation down somewhat to Sarah. If Milly told her about Henry pointing out what protection his name would give her, Sarah would probably insist on Milly marrying him! "It was an offer made for all the right reasons, but I couldn't force him to carry it through. It wouldn't be fair to any of us."

"It wasn't fair that you were discarded at the first sign of trouble by Connor, but you were! This would prevent you taking that job, and you would live in luxury for the rest of your days. Don't dismiss that the offer was made purely as a result of the situation you were both caught in. I don't think he's unaffected by you, Milly. I've seen the way he looks at you; it makes me feel quite hot and bothered his gaze is so intense!"

Milly laughed, "Oh Sarah you are such a sweetheart. Lord Grinstead could have the pick of the season, of any season! He is never going to be satisfied with me."

"I don't like that you don't see what the rest of us do, Milly. I'm sorry to say it, but I think you pay too much heed to what your mother says." Both women had witnessed Mrs Holland's caustic tongue, usually aimed at Milly, more so since her engagement had ended.

"He has agreed to do what I wish," Milly responded stubbornly. "There's nothing left to say."

The friends were left saddened by the visit that in other circumstances should have been such a joyous occasion.

*

Milly was not aware that Henry was not about to give in to what she wished without speaking to her once more. Admittedly, he was veering from abject panic at what he had done, to ridiculous contentment at the thought of having Milly permanently in his life; but he recognised there were more positives for them both if the marriage did take place.

He approached the Holland house with flowers and a basket of fruit. Mrs Holland greeted him like a long lost friend, promising to seek out Milly and leave them to have some time alone, unchaperoned. Henry smiled at the thought of being able to spend time kissing Milly instead of drinking tea.

Milly entered the room, for once feeling unsure and unprepared for what was to come; she had not expected to see Henry. Feeling drab in her striped cotton day dress, she admired his always perfect attire. Whatever time of day or night she saw him, his clothing was impeccable; she, on the other hand, always seemed to be mourning yet another crease or mark on her dress.

"Miss Holland, I'm delighted to find you in. I rode through the town before making my way here; I hoped to see you on your travels," Henry said, walking across and kissing her hand.

"I decided a shorter excursion was preferable this morning," Milly replied, moving to sit on a chair, but Henry, steered her to the two seater sofa. She wanted to have some distance from him, but it did not seem he shared the same thoughts.

"Your mother is being very amenable. I think she must approve of our match."

"Have you forgotten what we discussed before you made the announcement?" Milly asked wondering where this chipper Henry had come from.

"I thought that was just nerves of the moment. Surely my suit would be preferable than a position as companion in Ireland? I might be accused of thinking too highly of myself, but is it too egotistical to presume mine is the better offer?"

Henry spoke with such good-humour that Milly questioned if she was making the right decision. It would be so easy to go along with the scheme and just hope that they would be happy. Ultimately, though, she could not ignore the reality of the offer; accepting his proposal was not wise for either of them. "I haven't changed my mind, my lord," she said quietly, not meeting his eyes.

The air stilled between them, and Milly was forced to look at Henry. His face had clouded, his frown set firmly between his brows. "You are refusing me?"

"I refused you last night," Milly responded. "We would not make each other happy."

Henry stood, walking slightly away from Milly, running a hand through his hair. He turned to her in frustration. "If I promised the things you wanted last night? The faithfulness, and whatever other nonsense you uttered? What then?"

"The fact that you think it nonsense would make me doubtful of your commitment to any of the things I think are important." Milly couldn't help the slight smile touching her lips at his words.

"Do you realise I've never asked anyone else to marry me before?" Henry said in disbelief.

"As you are still single I would presume not."

"And you are turning me down."

"Yes, I'm sorry."

"It's an eligible offer!"

"It's for the best."

"Best for whom?"

"Both of us. I've no idea what you want in a wife, and it's clear that you don't know what I wish for in a husband. I'm releasing you from the engagement," Milly said. Her tone was quiet but firm.

"That just about explains everything!"

"What does? I don't understand your meaning?"

"You wouldn't release Connor, but you've been quick to release me! That shows exactly where your affection lies doesn't it? I've been a complete fool!" Henry snapped striding to the door. He was being unreasonable, but he could not overcome the jealousy towards Mr Connor. A man not used to feeling out of his depth was never going to react well when consumed with irrational jealousy for the first time in his life.

"Wait! No! You've misunderstood!" Milly cried, jumping from the seat and making to follow Henry.

"Have I? Have I really, Miss Holland? You wouldn't act to try and prevent some condemnation when dealing with that buffoon that you'd agreed to marry even when it meant you'd be subject to gossip, but you can't wait to break off the engagement to me! Don't worry! I won't be so foolish in the future; I accept the release and can only apologise for wishing for the union in the first place."

"Don't leave on these terms," Milly begged. She hated that he looked so hurt; she had never expected him to be so affected. The urge to wrap him in an embrace almost overwhelmed her.

"You can't agree to the terms I offered; there is no other way to part. I wish you good day, Miss Holland. I shall leave you to deal with the gossips as you see fit. You must be an expert at it by now!"

Henry stormed out of the house. He did not care that Mrs Holland would know that something was wrong; let Milly deal with her angry parent. He would leave this godforsaken part of the country; he had missed goodness knew how many other entertainments that London had to offer while he was stuck in this backwater. All thoughts of protecting her from Joshua Shambles were forgotten in the heat of the moment.

He had had his fill of Miss Holland and her high and mighty ideas. Wanting a faithful, loving marriage indeed! His parents had hardly been able to stay in the same room with each other, let alone care for one another. He had determined that he would never let anyone hurt him as they had hurt each other and here he was proposing to a woman so completely on the shelf that she had to move countries to gain suitable employ. Well she was on her own! Good riddance to her!

Chapter 12

Milly had managed to avoid her mother for a full day. Mrs Holland was busy visiting everyone to talk about her daughter's very eligible match. Claiming a headache, Milly had eaten small meals in her room and then retired early.

She had not lied; her head had been pounding since Henry stormed out of her home and, in all likelihood, her life. She went over and over what she had done but could not bring herself to acknowledge she had made a mistake. If she had agreed to the marriage he would break her heart, although if the way she was feeling at the moment was anything to go by, it had happened whether she had married him or not.

Crying and falling into a fitful sleep was not an ideal way to end a day, but it was the way her day ended. The following morning she forced herself out of her bedchamber and into the breakfast room. Mrs Holland entered soon afterwards, took one look at her daughter picking at her scones and dismissed the maid, closing the door firmly behind the member of staff.

"What has happened?" Mrs Holland demanded.

"I'm no longer engaged," Milly said dully. There was no point in trying to hide the truth, or lie about it.

With Henry leaving for London, if he had not gone already, she could not avoid her mother's censure.

If Milly expected an outburst, she was to be surprised; Mrs Holland sat down heavily on one of the solid dining room chairs. "Why not?"

"It was a mistake; it should never have been announced. Lord Grinstead was trying to save my reputation as Mr Connor had walked in and caught us sharing a kiss."

"So Lord Grinstead did the honourable thing."

"Yes, but it was wrong to tie ourselves to each other for the rest of our days just over one small kiss. I could not let him sacrifice his freedom for me."

"You foolish, foolish child!" Mrs Holland finally found her voice. "Do you realise what you've just thrown away? A secure future! I would give anything to have my remaining days secured, and instead I wake every morning thanking someone else's kindness for my position and hoping that it continues to last! Have you any idea what it is like to rely so much on others?"

"Of course I do!" Milly said indignantly. "I've spent the last four years with Clara."

"And been looked after as if you were a sister, not a penniless cousin! When you take up whatever position you decide on, things will be vastly different. You are staff then, not family and, believe me, there is a world of difference between the two!"

"A companion is not a maid," Milly responded, but her words lacked conviction.

"It's worse; in most cases, neither staff nor family. Milly, I've always thought you were intelligent, not one for dramatics, but you've just proved me wrong. You have successfully ruined any prospects of happiness you might have had and caused yourself to be the fool of the town. Can you imagine how this news will be received, especially after what went on with Mr Connor? Oh my goodness! The Connors will love this news!"

"I don't care about the Connors!"

"Well you should! They are the ones who are on the top tier of society in this town, whether we like it or not. They travel around, and won't they use this as a story to regale their friends with far and wide! You have just become notorious, and I can only pity the backlash you will feel as a result. The top families are all connected, the family you will go to will no doubt know someone who knows someone, and the story will reach them. Milly you have been a fool."

What shocked Milly about her mother's words was not their content, although that was bad enough; it was the fact that her mother had not shouted and screamed as Milly had expected. The words had been said with authority, but almost as if she pitied her daughter. It made the message hit its mark far more accurately than if the words had been said in anger.

"I thought I was acting in the best way for us both," Milly said quietly.

"He will be unaffected by this. Why should anyone fault him when he did the decent thing and offered for a woman he'd been seen kissing? In fact, he'll be applauded for his behaviour. It is you who will be at fault, not him. It is you who *is* at fault."

"I think I need to be outside," Milly responded, pushing her chair away from the table. "Please excuse me, Mother; I feel a little out of sorts; I need some fresh air."

Mrs Holland did not try to stop her daughter. Milly returned to her bedchamber to retrieve her pelisse and bonnet. She caught her reflection in her looking glass and was shocked at the pale ghost that looked back at her. For the first time she doubted her reasoning. What had she done?

*

Walking through the area known as The Bourne offered no relief for Milly. Thoughts jumbled into each other as one problem after another refused to be solved no matter how much she went over and over it in her mind.

Hours went by; Milly was exhausted, hungry and thirsty. She had to return home for some refreshments at least. As she walked towards the town and Castle Street, she wondered if Henry had already left for London. She did not suppose he would delay his return; after all she had been clear in her refusals.

Walking down a secluded path which opened onto a road that would lead her directly to the centre of town, she passed a young man who lifted his hat slightly as he passed her.

Milly nodded her response and thought no more of the boy, until she was grabbed from behind. A hand was placed firmly on her mouth and hot breath brushed her ear, whilst at the same time, she felt the sharp end of a blade in her ribs.

"Now Missy," came the rough voice. "One scream or noise and this blade gets more aquatinted with your ribs. Do I make myself clear?"

Milly nodded, and the hand was removed from her mouth. She felt a little sick, the hand had not been clean, and she could taste bitterness on her lips. The sharp edge at her side never let up in pressure.

"If you walk with me nice and easy like, your mama will be all fine and dandy, but if I don't pass by your abode in the next fifteen minutes in that coach over there, she'll be receiving a visit that'll be her last. Do you understand?"

Milly felt the blood drain from her face. "What are you going to do?"

"If you play nice, we pick up my friend who is waiting near your house, and we go on our merry way. If I don't get there, well, let's just say, you and those little brothers of yours will all be orphans today, and that's not a nice thought is it?"

"Are my brothers safe?" Milly cried, panic rising in her chest.

"They will be if you're no trouble."

"I'll do anything you say; please don't hurt my family."

"That's what I like to hear," came the smiling response.

The young man led Milly to the waiting coach; its driver was already seated, controlling the two horses. Milly never made a murmur as she entered the carriage even though her hands and legs were shaking so much that her kidnapper had to help her into the body of the carriage. He nodded to the driver and climbed in beside Milly.

Locking the door, the man smiled. "I don't want any funny business while we're travelling."

"I've given you my word," Milly responded, her voice was slightly shaky, but she appeared calm. "As long as you promise that my family is safe, you have my co-operation."

"Knew you'd be a good 'un," he said with approval. "We're going to be spending some time together over these next few days, so you'd best be calling me Billy; everyone else does."

"Where are we going?" Milly was astute enough to realise this had something to do with Joshua Shambles, but she was not going to ask too many questions at once.

"It doesn't matter; just be a good 'un and all will be well. Settle yourself down, Missy, we're going to be travelling a long while."

*

Henry sat in the bar in the Hogs Back Inn. He had already delayed leaving for a day, spending most of the previous day in a drunken stupor in his room. He had been angry leaving Castle Street, but it had soon turned to self-pity. He was not able to acknowledge the depth of his feelings for Milly, never having experienced anything like them previously; but he was terribly out of sorts.

He had managed to sleep off the previous day's excesses, moving to the public bar area with the intention of starting on his journey to London. If he wanted to visit Castle Street once more before he left Surrey he was not yet ready to admit it, so he stayed in a state of limbo drinking brandy, which was probably smuggled he thought ironically to himself.

Sarah and Peter walked into the inn, noticing Henry immediately. Sarah was surprised to see the usually impeccable Lord, looking somewhat disarrayed. His clothing was creased, his face unshaven, his hair unstyled. It was a state she hoped was a good sign about his feelings for Milly.

Peter took the lead, speaking to the innkeeper before approaching Henry. When he had secured a private parlour, he walked over to where Henry was seated. "My lord, would you be good enough to spare me a moment of your time?"

"Hastings? What can you want from me?"

"I'd rather we speak in private, my lord."

"I'm comfortable here," Henry said belligerently. He had noticed Sarah and wondered if Milly had sent her friend. If she had, he was not about to make it easy for the chit.

"Please, my lord," Peter said quietly.

"Oh, for goodness sake!" Sarah said exasperated. Now was not the time for pandering to men who should know better. "Move into the parlour now, my lord! Time for nonsense is passed; my friend is missing!"

Henry became suddenly more sober but then slumped. "Look at the ships leaving for Ireland. She seemed determined to do as she'd planned."

Sarah leaned closer to Henry. "Unless you want me to have a bout of hysterics right here and now, I suggest you follow me without further delay into the private room, *my lord*. Stop acting the self-pitying wastrel!"

Henry stared at the woman in disbelief at her tone and words. He looked at Peter who had almost choked at Sarah's words and shrugged apologetically at Henry. "There must be something in the bloody water here that makes all the women turn into fishwives," Henry muttered, but he moved off the stool that had been his support for a number of hours and followed Sarah into the private parlour.

The parlour was clean, if a little bare: just a table, chairs and bench near the window with a side table near the lit fireplace. It was an area for a fixed purpose: providing privacy for food and drink rather than fighting through crowds in the main room then moving the occupants on to make the maximum use of the room.

Sarah did not sit but stood in front of the brick fireplace. "I'm presuming you haven't seen Milly in these last two days?" There was no point in trying to pretend the visit was to exchange niceties; it was not.

"I've had quite my fill of Miss Holland after visiting her at her home the day before yesterday. I'm the last person she would want to see," Henry responded, his tone cool and aloof.

"I'm not arguing about that fact at the moment, but you are completely wrong. More importantly, Milly is missing."

Henry took a while to process the words, but turning to Sarah, it was clear which words his alcohol befuddled mind had focused on. "Why am I wrong? Did I not hear her repeated refusal? I think you don't know your friend too well if she hasn't told you what happened between us. She preferred the suit of that idiot Connor to mine!"

"Oh, for goodness sake!" Sarah groaned. "You foolish man! She is completely in love with you! Connor was a young infatuation; she would never have been happy with him. She didn't realise the truth of that until she met you though! You are the one she adores!"

"And yet she refused me? I'm not convinced of your argument, Mrs Hastings. It is completely flawed," came the derisive reply.

"Because she thought that your feelings were unmoved. She couldn't risk being hurt when you took a mistress or whatever the aristocracy does to each other when they marry! Thank goodness I married a sensible man who hasn't addled his brain through drink!" Sarah responded tartly.

Henry looked dumbfounded. "Really? She thought I didn't care?"

"Really! Now can we get back to the real reason for our visit?" Sarah continued. "Milly is missing. She isn't due to meet with her new employer for nearly a sennight and none of her belongings have gone. Just her."

Finally, the words sank into his consciousness, and Henry sobered in an instant. "Where was she last seen and when?"

"She was seen walking near The Bourne, an area a little way out of town but not far enough that she hasn't been there a thousand times before. She never returned home. At first Mrs Holland thought she was spending the day with me, so she only sent a message to our house late last night. We've been trying to trace her movements all morning. We can't understand why she would have gone missing and can only presume that she has been taken ill somewhere."

"Good God! He's got her from right under my nose!" Henry said, banging his hands on the table in frustration.

"Who has?"

"It's a long story. I need to return to London."

Peter stepped in before Henry had a chance to leave the room. "We need more of an explanation. I can't return to Mrs Holland with such little information. She is understandably worried."

"Blast it!" Henry cursed. He quickly told them of the events that had taken place at Dorset and his subsequent request of Milly and the consequences of that.

"So you think this Shambles has taken her?" Sarah asked; all earlier bravado disappeared when facing the reality of her friend being in danger. "Milly did mention about the drawing, but I admit I didn't take it seriously. I thought you were over reacting. Would he travel here to reach her?"

"Definitely," Henry responded grimly.

"You put her in danger. You put her family in danger. How can she possibly have feelings for you after doing that? I don't understand," Sarah said in confusion.

"I wasn't convinced she had; it was you who told me her feelings weren't untouched as I'd presumed from her behaviour," Henry pointed out not unreasonably.

"How can you do a job that puts others so much at risk?"

Henry was reminded of another time before he had accepted his current occupation when life had seemed far simpler. He shook himself; now was not for dwelling on what had already passed. "It protects the rest of the country. There is a real threat from France. I couldn't stand by and see Napoleon invade."

"But it's put Milly in danger."

"I need to return to London. He'll be taking her there."

"She will never be found in London!" Sarah gasped.

"If I have to tear every brick from every building, I'll find her," Henry said fiercely. If he had felt fear at Milly being hurt previously, it was nothing compared to the feelings of terror he was desperately trying to dampen down in order that he could think straight. "Please excuse me; I need to send off some correspondence before I start my journey. A search for her can be started before I return to London."

Sarah reached out and touched Henry's arm. "You will find her?"

"I promise."

Chapter 13

Milly was exhausted. They had travelled with hardly a break. She had been allowed to leave the carriage only once when she had been forced to explain that, if she was not allowed to leave, there would be unpleasant consequences for anyone travelling inside. It had been one of the most embarrassing experiences of her life but, unfortunately, necessary.

Having a young man standing outside a room while she freshened up had been a necessary evil. There had been no opportunity to try to make an escape; the room had been checked before she had been allowed access, and the window was small enough that even she could not have hoped to squeeze through.

Milly had considered for a moment trying to escape, a natural instinct to flee, but it was not a possibility in reality. Billy had informed her of the address of the school her brothers were attending; at that moment Milly had assured them once more of her co-operation, and she had not changed her mind. She could not risk this unfortunate event impacting any other member of her family.

She had agreed to draw the picture of Joshua Shambles mainly out of vanity, and it just served herself right that she had not considered the consequences of becoming involved with something that was so obviously dangerous. It was ironic that not so very long ago she had berated Henry for putting people at risk, yet she had put her whole family at risk. She was thankful that her cousins were still on their wedding trip and could not be drawn into this mess.

A lesser person would have blamed Henry for her current position but, although Milly acknowledged he had involved her, she had been a willing participant. To be fair to Henry, he had remained near her in Farnham when he had heard Joshua had found out who was behind the drawings. He had promised her protection and, in fairness, he had given it, even to the point of the silly marriage proposal.

Milly grimaced as the coach continued to trundle along even though it was dark; they were obviously not afraid of being approached by highwaymen as most other travellers were. Normally travel at night would be avoided for fear of being attacked on the road; this was clearly not a consideration on this journey. She was sure they were returning to London, but what would happen when they reached the capital, she could only guess at.

In moments of despair, she wondered if Joshua would kill her for what she had done. It was clear he had gone to a lot of trouble to ensure her capture. There was another thought that had sprung into her mind as the day had progressed, but that thought did not bear thinking of. She prayed that Henry would not be put in danger because of trying to find her.

It was late when Milly was roused from a fitful sleep by the halting of the carriage. It took a moment or two before she realised it was not a normal horse-changing stop, but that they'd entered a dock area. Milly was surprised at the level of noise surrounding them even though the hour was late; it was clear that the docks did not sleep as the more elegant streets did.

She was instructed to put on a long cloak and put the hood over her head. Doing as she was bid, stepping out the carriage, she turned to Billy who was, as always, watching her closely.

"What happens now?"

"That's not up to me Missy; my job was to get you here. I'm paid and then off on my way," Billy responded, his hand leading Milly by her elbow into a large warehouse. They walked through a building full of barrels and boxes of all shapes and sizes. Milly wondered if there could be so much illegal goods without any authority figure noticing; there was such a large amount, but the law must be looking the other way as she did not think anything to do with Joshua Shambles would be legitimate.

A section of the warehouse had been partitioned off from the large open space, and Billy rapped on the door. It was opened slightly while the visitors were checked. A second later, the door was opened fully, allowing the pair access into the room.

Milly was faced with two men, one of whom was Joshua Shambles. She stopped the sharp intake of breath before it was heard when she saw the ugly scar on his cheek. It had not healed well and was an horrific sight to anyone but especially to a genteel young woman. She knew without question who had inflicted the scar, and the feeling of dread increased ten-fold in her chest. Joshua was not going to be inclined to be lenient with his treatment of her when he had such a disfigurement caused by her own cousin.

"Had a good look?" Joshua sneered. "This'll be nothing by the time I'm finished with you."

"Have you my money?" Billy asked, obviously not keen to hang around now he had delivered his part of the deal.

Joshua threw him a bag that jangled with coins. Billy caught the cloth bag and weighed it in his hand. "Nice doing business with you."

"Any word of you talking about this, and I'll cut your tongue out," Joshua snarled at Billy.

Milly almost laughed when Billy turned and doffed his cap at her in deference before leaving the room. He had been pointing a knife at her for most of the journey; it was ironic to now be so subservient.

Milly turned back to face Joshua when the door closed behind Billy. She was terrified but needed to know answers to some questions. "I don't need to ask why I'm here, but what do you intend to do to me now?" she asked. Her voice was slightly shaky, but it was something she could not have stopped; she was no gothic heroine.

"Oh, so you admit your part in trying to see me hanged?"

"You nearly got my cousins killed; you tried to get yourself hanged."

Joshua moved quicker than Milly thought possible, the back of his hand across her face sent her reeling to the floor. She gasped in pain, unable to stop the tears but managing to contain her sobs.

"I expect respect while you're under my roof!" Joshua snapped.

"Josh, damaged goods won't get you the result you want." It was the first time the other man had spoken, and his voice was quiet.

"I'm sick of the likes of her talking down to me! I had enough while I stayed with her fop of a cousin!" Joshua snapped.

"It's up to you, but you know full well how they are about their women being untouched."

Joshua pulled Milly to her feet. She flinched, expecting another blow, but it didn't come. "You, Miss High and Mighty are my ticket out of this mess. I'm swapping you for a pardon. Your Lord Grinstead will be given the choice: your life or my freedom. Easy as that."

Milly was flung onto a pile of what turned out to be empty hessian sacks. "You stay here quiet, and you'll be safe. If you cause a noise, I won't hesitate to bring one of your brothers to join you. Do you understand?"

Milly nodded, mute.

"Good. There'll be someone watching this door day and night. If you're no trouble I might feed you. Maybe but maybe not; we'll see."

Joshua and the second man walked out of the door and locked it. Milly sank back on the sacking, touching her face tenderly. She could taste blood, and her cheek felt sore; there would probably be a bruise but, as the way she looked was definitely the least of her worries, she let her head fall back on the rough material. She could not think straight, but one thought would not go away; it was unlikely she would get out of this unscathed, if at all. Staring at the closed door, she knew the next few hours or days were going to be the most testing of her life.

*

The door opened, and Milly sat up quickly. During the night she had arranged the sacking into a more comfortable arrangement, even using one as a blanket. The cloak she had been given protected her from most of the roughness of the material, and it had enabled her to get some sleep, even though she still felt weary on being woken.

She looked in alarm at the door, expecting to see Joshua, but it was the second man who walked in with a tray in his hands. "Here you go, Miss Holland. It's not fine fare, but it should fill a hole."

"Thank you," Milly said quietly. "What should I do about...?" her cheeks had flushed at needing to raise the issue for the second time in two days, both times with men.

The man smiled in sympathy. "This cupboard contains everything you need, and if you leave the door open, the door acts as a screen."

"How long will I be here?" Milly asked.

"It depends what your Lord intends to do."

"He dislikes Mr Shambles."

"Aye, there's not many who do like him."

"Then why?" Milly asked in confusion. "Why would he get co-operation from everyone if they did not respect him?"

"Money, usually. Don't ask too many questions. None of us can afford to be your friend, Miss Holland, for all our sakes." The words were said gently, but there was a warning.

"I hate being so helpless," Milly admitted.

"Just don't antagonise him, and you'll be fine."

"Am I allowed to ask your name?"

"Everyone calls me Mack. Now eat your food; it'll taste even worse cold."

"Thank you, Mack."

Milly stood and stretched her stiff muscles. She was not used to such inactivity and spending too many hours in a carriage and then an uncomfortable night did not bode well for the days to come. She looked at the food on the tray; Mack had been correct; it was anything but fine fare. A slice of pie with thick, dry-looking pastry lay on its side. A few unappetising biscuits completed the offered food, and a jug of small beer was the only drink on the tray.

Having been so long without food—only once on the journey had food been obtained, and that had been eaten in the carriage—Milly was ready to eat almost anything. Taking small bites and washing the stale food down with the now much appreciated drink, Milly did indeed fill a hole.

When she had finished, she felt less drained and walked backwards and forwards across the small floor of the locked room. She hated being so helpless and unable to change anything about her current situation, but the risk for her family was enough of a deterrent to prevent her from doing anything rash. She was not about to underestimate Joshua Shambles' determination to seek vengeance. She would have to wait for the moment. Doing nothing was not a perfect solution, but there was little else she could do.

*

Milly had suffered three days of staring at the same walls, walking around the small confined room and eating dried, tasteless food, washed down with small beer, vital to help swallow the dry morsels. She had never liked the taste of small beer, but she was positively grateful for it now.

Mack had been the one to visit each time food was delivered. She had tried to delay him by asking questions and, although he was in some respects kindly to her, he never loitered above a minute or two. Milly craved contact with someone; she was desperately hoping her family were safe, and that Joshua would get what he wanted without her ever needing to see him again.

In the hours of silence Milly thought of Henry, wondering what he was doing, hoping he was safe and, more often than not, hoping he could forgive her pushing him away. She ached to see him again but was terrified he would risk his safety in searching for her. She presumed there would be some agreement being worked out for Joshua's pardon.

The morning of the fourth day, the door burst open, and Joshua stormed into the room. "I knew that damned Earl wouldn't be a gentleman and do things the easy way! Get up! We're leaving."

Milly was unceremoniously dragged to her feet and pushed forcefully through the door.

"What's happening?" she asked, partly relieved to be leaving the room behind, partly fearful of what was going to happen with Joshua in such a foul mood.

"You need to be moved somewhere more secure," Joshua snarled. "Now keep quiet, or there'll be more bruises!"

Milly instinctively touched her cheek which was less tender than it had been but was obviously bruised.

She received a look of warning from Mack that stopped her from asking any other questions.

She was dragged through the warehouse, her feet tripping regularly. She was shocked at how stiff she was and how it was causing her to struggle to walk at speed even after such a short confinement. Joshua cursed at every stumble and gripped her harder until she could hardly feel anything but the sharp pain in her arms where his fingers dug deeply into her flesh.

They reached the large doorway, and a carriage that had seen better days was waiting. Milly was lifted roughly and thrown into the open doorway of the carriage. She landed on the floor with a groan but soon scrambled onto the seat as Joshua and Mack followed her inside.

The carriage set-off before Mack had time to close the door, and a curse from the quiet man rang out as he reached for the swinging door.

"I'm sure there's no need for quite so much rush," he muttered to Joshua.

"Wait until it's your neck in the noose, and then we'll see how fast you move!" Joshua snapped in return.

"They'll hardly hand me a reward for my part in all this," Mack said with a nod towards Milly. "I signed up for getting people into the country, not kidnapping ladies."

"Well things changed because of them, not me." Joshua's tone was mulish; he never accepted responsibility for anything that happened; the situations he found himself in were never his fault if there was someone else to blame. "Why he couldn't just agree to my terms! This could all be over now!"

"And let a commoner get one over on an aristocrat? What foolish ideas you have sometimes!" Mack almost laughed at the young man. "We are in this mess because the toffs always get what they think they're entitled to."

"So the quicker we can bring them down the better."

"Only you'll have to do it even more carefully. If they pardon you, you'll be watched like a hawk," Mack pointed out.

"There's plenty others to take my place."

"And me?"

"Don't worry, I'll put you in touch with those who'd appreciate your skills. There's a gap in the organisation since that fiasco in Dorset," Joshua said, referring to the night that Milly had thought her cousins had been killed. "To lose so many men that night and in the days after has been a blow. You'll receive a faster promotion."

"That's good."

Milly was surprised that Joshua had spoken so openly in front of her and could only come to one depressing conclusion as to the reason for it. She was seen as expendable, so it did not matter what she heard; she was not going to survive long enough to tell anyone. She wondered if Joshua did not believe he would receive a pardon; surely he would not go to so much trouble if he did not?

The thought was unwelcome for one so constrained in what she could do, but the overriding thought that Milly had was that she would never see Henry again, and they had parted on such poor terms. How she wanted to be able to right the ill-feeling between them, but it was too late.

They rode through the dock areas. Milly was able to look out of the window and, although the areas were busy with activity, there were signs of squalor that she had not known existed. Children were barefoot and shoddily clothed. Some actually looked as if they were living in the gutter. They were dirty beyond anything she had ever seen, and her heart twisted at the bleak expressions on their faces.

Men were at work everywhere; she glimpsed ships being unloaded and loaded, warehouses being filled with produce for onward journeys into the capital and beyond. The work looked dirty and hard; clothes were filthy and torn in some cases. The men swore and shouted, making the whole area explode with noise as the constant movement of boxes, barrels and crates was combined with the cacophony of voices.

It was part fascinating, part disturbing. The only women that Milly saw were one or two loitering in the area of the occasional ale house they passed. From the garish clothing they wore, Milly was under no doubt that they would start work later in the day when the main harbour-related work had ended.

Milly shrank back in her seat; she might be eight and twenty, but she knew this landscape would swallow her without a trace even if there was the opportunity to escape. This was not an area that would provide her with the freedom she longed for. It seemed as if she were moving further into the bowels of hell, and the possibility of returning to her old life seemed less and less likely.

The carriage came to a stop at the edge of a building where work was going on; it was no surprise that the ever busy docks were constantly expanding. The fact that they had stopped in an area that was not yet fully developed made the area less busy than a working dock and, when Milly alighted from the carriage, she was led into a building that was only partly built.

Behind one door a set of stone stairs was revealed, which Milly was roughly led down and then dragged into a room which contained a door that could be locked. This was a far different prospect than her previous prison, and Milly shuddered at the thought of being locked inside this dank cell.

The walls were made of stone, the doorway being hewed out of solid stone. The cellar was necessary to take the weight of the tall building that was emerging, stretching its tall, dark walls towards the sky. The only light was provided by a small opening at the top of the outside wall, but nothing could be seen of the outside. A table and two chairs set in the middle with a hard bunk along one side and a hole in the floor in one corner all indicated that any previous use was likely to have been as a holding cell of some sort. Whether it was the intention, after the building was finished, that some poor souls would be held before being transported, there was no way to know. However it was to be used it was clear there would be nothing of a pleasant nature connected to the room.

Milly tried to talk herself into having courage to face a stay in this prison, but she knew she was visibly trembling. Joshua looked at her and smiled. "Not so confident now, eh? Let's see what you're like after a night spent with the rats."

"Please, could I have a candle?" Milly asked her voice shaking at the thought of the darkness that would descend when daylight faded.

"Ha! Not a chance! Mack she's all yours to sort out. I've got business to see to that I should have done at the beginning of all this."

Joshua and Mack left the cell, locking the door behind them. Milly stood in the centre of the room, her arms wrapped tightly around her waist, trying to talk herself into being brave; something that seemed an unlikely occurrence in her present situation.

Mack found Milly in the same position when he entered the room half an hour later and sighed to himself. The poor girl was probably terrified, but she had not broken down. He could see the struggle she was having with herself, and he cursed to himself; there were too many times that innocent people were hurt in all of this, and he was sick of being witness to it.

"See here, there's candles, matches, and blankets. I'll bring food and drink later. Try not to worry."

"I don't wish to sound overly dramatic, but I'm struggling with trying not to be overcome at the thought of spending the night with goodness knows how many rats!"

Mack smiled slightly. "I'll see what I can do to help."

Milly forced herself to move and set up a bed of sorts. This room felt different than the previous one; it was far damper and had a permanent chill; she was certain the night was going to be long and hard.

The day dragged for Milly. She had not realised what comfort the first room had been in comparison to the one she now occupied. The cold seemed to seep into her bones as the day wore on. Only when the light became too dim did she light a candle, frightened of using too many in case there was a limited supply.

Mack returned, as promised, with another young man who Milly had never seen before. She sat quietly on the bunk as Mack issued instructions to the younger man who was carrying in a number of items. Mack placed a tray of food and drink on the table and then indicated that he should be left alone with Milly. The door closed firmly as the helper exited, and Milly turned her gaze onto Mack.

"Joshua will probably skin me alive if he finds out I've been so soft with you, but I couldn't have you dying of a chill on my conscience," Mack said in his quiet, lilting voice.

"I appreciate all your kindnesses," Milly assured him.

"But I've not been overly kind and set you free have I? Don't overestimate my good deed."

"Candles are a huge help," Milly reasoned.

"This board, I'll put over the petty," Mack said.

"Petty?" Milly asked, being unfamiliar with the term.

"It's the place to do your business. We call it petty where I come from," Mack explained. He moved a large, heavy piece of wood until it covered the hole in the corner. "Rats would come up that way."

Milly shuddered. "What about the hole acting as a window?"

"I've brought this; that should put them off coming in that way," Mack explained, dragging a wrought iron brazier near the wall. "I'll bring some wood and a bit of coal so you can have a fire; it won't be ideal, there isn't a draught to pull the smoke up through the hole, but it might work and help keep the rats at bay as well as providing a bit of heat."

"Thank you."

Mack nodded and left the room before returning with the promised fuel for the fire. He made a small fire in the brazier and, although there was a lot of smoke to start with, he hoped that it would settle down. "I'll check you in a short while; I don't want the smoke causing you to choke to death."

"No. I suppose at the moment I'm still useful to Joshua." Milly had stopped using Joshua's title and family name, she did not think he deserved the respect.

"Yes, you are, and I hope for all our sakes he gets a pardon soon."

"What will happen if he doesn't?"

"He'll become more desperate than he is now, and that isn't good for anyone."

Mack left Milly to eat her chunk of bread and slices of ham. There was quite a bit of smoke, but it was not unbearable; Milly suspected the opening had been used as a chimney previously as there was a blackening of the wall where Mack had placed the brazier. So, even though the warehouse was not completed, the prison had been used; Milly shuddered at the thought.

The door opened, and Mack entered carrying more fuel. "Everything well?" he asked, collecting the tray.

"Yes, thank you."

"Try and sleep; you could be here for some time."

Milly lit another candle when she lost the light outside. The brazier provided a lot of light, but, just for the first night, she needed the extra comfort the candle would bring. If Mack's prediction was correct, she would need to conserve the candles, firewood and small pieces of coal. She stayed awake until she could not keep her eyes open any longer. She had no idea of the time but knew it must be the early hours of the morning. Not wanting the fire to die down when it was more likely that rats were active—out exploring the area to see what food they could forage before the world became busy with people once more—had kept Milly awake far beyond what she would have normally been.

Finally unable to resist sleep any longer, she wrapped herself in the musty smelling blankets and fell into a deeper sleep than she had expected on her arrival in her new prison.

*

Noise and movement startled Milly into wakefulness with her expecting to be faced with rats with large boots on, but it did not take too long to realise that it was human noise that had disturbed her slumber so forcefully.

It took Milly a few seconds before she blinked into consciousness to take in the scene. Joshua and another man were dragging a tethered form into the room. They were kicking the object as they pulled it along.

As soon as the form had been dragged far enough into the room, Joshua stood up, breathing deeply. He turned to Milly. "Your rescuer has failed, Miss Holland. I'm going to have to decide what to do with you both now. It's an interesting quandary I'm faced with; I doubt I'll get a pardon now, but I need to work out which of you will get me off these shores and which of you I should feed to the fishes, because I certainly won't need you both!"

Milly looked in horror at Joshua, which seemed to delight him. He aimed one last kick at the still form on the floor before leaving the cell. Milly let out a breath of relief; Joshua had been so concerned with inflicting pain and gloating he had not noticed the remains of the fire or the candles.

She quickly climbed off the bunk and crouched next to the form. Her heart stilled as she realised whose bloody body was lying still on the cold stone floor.

Milly moaned in despair. "No! No! No!" she keened as she touched Henry's still form.

Chapter 14

Henry had never travelled as speedily to London as he did knowing Milly was in danger. He had thought once before that he would never feel as bad again, but he was to realise that thought was incorrect. If anything happened to Milly…. He had urged his horse on as a feeling of panic travelled through his body.

When he arrived home tired and dishevelled, he was relieved to receive replies to the messages he had sent express before he had left the inn. It meant the network was fully aware of Milly's disappearance, and hopefully news would be received of her location soon.

He paid a visit to Bow Street. As a spy of the Home Office, he would not normally work with Bow Street, but he had not used every avenue once before to his sorrow, and he was not about to make that mistake again. After a successful meeting, he returned home confident that there were a large number of people looking for Milly.

Henry had always worked on the more salubrious side of society, leaving the seedier side to his friend Edmund and others. The first night home, though, he donned appropriate formal wear and explored every venue he could get round to in an effort to see if anything could be gleaned from those who were more eager to talk after enough drink had been consumed.

He arrived home when the sun was high in the sky without having gained enough knowledge to lead him in the right direction. He had heard Shambles was not happy about being hounded since he had discovered the existence of the picture. As this was old news to Henry it did not advance his search.

The third day of frustrated searching, speaking to anyone who might be able to help, and some whom he would have previously avoided at all costs, brought him home tired, sweaty and in a foul mood caused by the feeling of helplessness descending on him.

He ordered a bath and retired to his study where his butler followed him. "This letter arrived about an hour ago, m'lord. A young boy insisted you should receive it the moment you returned home."

Henry accepted the letter and once he was left alone he sat on his captain's chair and broke the seal.

If you want to see Miss Holland again, I suggest you follow the instructions contained in this letter. Any evidence of not doing exactly as I demand, and she will not live to celebrate another birthday.

I want a full pardon, I want it published in the papers. You will be able to arrange it if you try hard enough. It needs to happen soon; because of the amount of those damned pictures floating around with a price on my head, I can't trust anyone. The reward is too great. I want to come out of the shadows. When I've seen the advertisement in all the newspapers, I'll send a message, and your little artist will be released. If my message ain't received I promise she won't be doing any more pretty pictures.

Don't doubt my word. I've nothing to lose. I will carry out my threat.

Joshua Shambles.

Henry crumpled the letter, slamming his hand on the leather arm of the chair. Joshua was going to use Milly to gain a pardon and not face the consequences for anything he had done now or in the past. He could not get away with it. Even if Henry agreed to the terms, there was no guarantee that, once out of danger, Joshua would keep his word and release her. She was in such a precarious situation it made his stomach turn.

*

Over the following two days Henry increased his efforts in trying to find Milly's location. He did everything in his power but was exhausted and frustrated at the end of the second day because he was gaining no ground.

It was late evening when his butler knocked on his study door and announced that a Mr King wished to have an audience with him.

Henry agreed to the visit even though he was travel weary and tired. As under-secretary at the Home Office, King could have news. The portly man was shown into Henry's study and accepted a glass of brandy.

Henry looked at the man who carried out quite a bit of groundwork for the powers that be, even though he was under-secretary and could have remained office bound. He had been in government for many of his seven and forty years and had seen many upheavals as a result.

"An unexpected visit," Henry started.

"Is it?" came the pleasant response. "You've been causing quite a ruckus over these last few days."

"With no results to speak of."

"You've managed to upset many people, including Mr Shambles."

"And yet he still has Miss Holland captive," Henry said bitterly.

"The powers that be need you to rethink your strategy."

"Why?"

"You are risking the lives of some of our operatives who are working deep undercover. I don't need to remind you how hazardous their position is."

"Equally as perilous as Miss Holland's situation I presume."

"We have been trying to find out for a long time who are the leaks in the higher echelons of society. After the business at Dorset, young Shambles has been promoted up the ranks, purely because his superiors were either killed or transported because of you. It turned out to be a fortuitous turn of events. We are that much closer now, and this opportunity is too important to be lost because of one unknown spinster with few connections," Mr King explained.

Henry was reminded of a conversation with Edmund that had occurred a few months previously when he had suggested that Edmund use the then Miss Baker to achieve his goal. Edmund had been angry then and accused Henry of being cold and unfeeling and not considering who he stepped on to achieve his goal. Edmund had probably had feelings for Miss Baker as early as that by the way he reacted. Henry could not condemn his friend; he was fully aware that currently he was having feelings deeper than he had ever experienced before, and it was driving him onward until he was completely exhausted. It had just taken time before Edmund had admitted to his feelings. He wondered if he would ever be able to acknowledge openly his own feelings.

"I cannot leave her to face her fate alone. She is in this situation because of me," Henry confessed. Any hint of his affection would cause him to lose all credibility in the eyes of Mr King.

"It wasn't your fault what happened with— "

"Was it not?" Henry said bitterly. "It was my job to protect her and, because I was off having a good time, she was left vulnerable to be easily preyed on."

"He's good at his job; she didn't have a chance."

"He's not going to take another young life."

"You risk your own in the process. I can't give any guarantees of support if you should need it," Mr King said, his tone severe in his effort to convince what he saw as headstrong behaviour.

"That's a risk I shall have to take," Henry responded stubbornly. He could not, he would not leave Milly to face her fate alone.

"Then there's no more to discuss is there, really?" Mr King said, standing. "I wish you safety on your fool's errand, but be assured we won't let you risk our operatives."

"I was once considered an operative. It's interesting how soon a situation can change," Henry said wryly.

"If you are putting good men's lives at risk, they come first; they face danger every day."

"I'm glad to have that cleared up before I catch up with Shambles; I shan't have the same compunction that I would have had about killing him when I was considered one of you."

"You can't do that! He holds information we need!"

"He holds a woman who I need and, if to secure her safety, it means I kill Shambles, so be it."

"This is why we should never consider using anyone with a title; you're too bloody full of your own self-importance! You never listen to reason!" Mr King said angrily.

Henry smiled. "Of which until now, you've been grateful. My butler will see you out, King. I bid you goodnight; I doubt our paths will cross again."

Henry waited until the door had closed behind Mr King before rubbing his hands over his face. He was on his own; he just hoped that was enough to save Milly.

*

Henry had written a long letter to Edmund before setting out on his quest. He had received a note an hour previously that had finally given his search some direction, and it was important that he trust someone with the details of what he was intending. If all went wrong, his body would likely be found somewhere downstream in the Thames. He was not overly concerned about his safety, but he wanted someone to continue the search for Milly.

The note had simply read; *Shambles is angry with the upheaval you are causing. Your package is contained in a partially built warehouse in the Surrey Docks.*

The Surrey Docks was an area of expansion in the dock area. It was in the region of Rotherhithe; as trade routes continued to expand, so did the docks. Henry was to explore an area he was not familiar with, but he had run out of options.

He armed himself with knives, two pistols and a cane. There would be a fight, and he had to try to prepare for every eventuality; any small advantage could pay dividends.

He left his house, taking a hackney as far as he could before he set off on foot into the dark night. He hoped to goodness the building would be easy to identify; otherwise it would be a long night of searching partially built buildings.

Henry's coachman's greatcoat covered his more expensive coat, but even the quality of the greatcoat made a few people watch the stranger passing through the area late at night. Most wondered how far he would get in the dangerous location before someone challenged him, but one or two figures disappeared into the shadows sure they had seen the man who Shambles always seemed to be ranting about and who if seen they would receive a reward for information.

As Henry systematically examined each building, entering some but not all, he was unaware that he was soon to be reunited with Milly but not in the way he expected.

*

"So, the great Lord Grinstead comes to visit," came the clear, sneering voice of Joshua Shambles as he stepped from the shadows.

Henry halted, his hand instinctively moving to the hilt of one of his knives. "Where is she?"

"Oh, far from your grasp," Joshua mocked. A nod of his head caused a number of figures to emerge from the shadows, surrounding Henry. "You haven't been introduced to my friends, have you?"

With the words Joshua nodded and stepped back in one fluid movement, and Henry was hit from behind. He managed to swing around and land a blow before he felt the next blow reach its target. He dragged his knife out and one small pistol, shooting one of the attackers. It seemed that the action did not gain any advantage as another figure filled the gap caused by the first attacker crumpling to the ground.

Henry fought as he had never fought before but eight to one were not fair odds, and it was not very long before he had been knocked to his knees and then sent sprawling on the floor. When his body was still, Joshua stepped forward once more.

"Enough, boys!" Joshua said, with a whistle to catch the attention of the thugs intent on finishing the job they had started. "His final breath is to be at my hands, not yours. Here, you've earned your wages tonight." He took out a bag of money from his pocket and handed out a large number of coins. He considered the money well spent.

When only Joshua and Mack remained, Joshua turned to his loyal member of staff. "A pity he isn't conscious enough to walk. I don't fancy carrying him, but I should have thought of that earlier. I was enjoying the sight of his bloody face being beaten to a pulp too much to stop matters earlier. Come, give me a hand; he's a heavy brute."

Chapter 15

Milly had checked for signs of life and had nearly wept with relief when she felt shallow breaths on her hand when she held it in front of his lips. He had been badly beaten; bruises were already emerging.

She tried to lift him off the cold floor but could barely lift one side of him; she could never move him without help. Looking around the small cell in desperation, she covered him with a blanket and her cloak, but it was not enough; he needed to be off the floor.

Milly had been the model prisoner, but circumstances had changed. She stood at the door and banged with all her might, shouting for help at the same time.

It was many minutes before Milly heard the sound of the door being unlocked and stepped away from the doorway, rubbing her now bruised hand. Her heart beat uncomfortably in her chest as she dreaded the sight of Joshua.

Mack entered the room and closed the door firmly behind him. "What do you think you're doing?" he asked roughly.

"Lord Grinstead needs help."

"He's lucky he's still alive, the young fool," Mack sounded angry.

Milly decided that she had to have faith in Mack; he had helped her so much already. "Please help me lift him on the bed. He'll catch a chill if he remains on the floor."

Mack muttered under his breath but bent to haul Henry's upper body onto the hard bunk. Milly quickly grabbed his feet and was relieved Henry was off the stone floor.

"I need something to clean his wounds," Milly said, her eyes pleading with Mack's steely glare.

"You're asking too much."

"Please. He must've been trying to find me; I can't see him hurt without helping him."

"He's put you both in real danger," Mack responded.

"We'll deal with that when the time comes. I'd already accepted that I probably wouldn't be leaving here alive," Milly said, her tone matter-of-fact.

Mack looked at the young woman and, with a small smile, showed his appreciation of her spirit. "I'll bring what I can but, when he comes to, it'll be up to you to keep him quiet. Antagonising Joshua at this point won't be a good idea."

"I'll do my best. He's probably never followed anyone's advice in his life, but I'll try."

Milly would never have guessed the level of respect Mack had for the woman who had dealt with her confinement with the utmost dignity and lack of complaint. Even now, when he could tell by the look in her eyes that she was terrified, she maintained her composure and tried to make a bleak situation better. It was wrong that she was being put through such a trial.

An hour passed before Mack returned. Milly had been afraid he would not bring the items to tend to Henry, so she had lit the fire and one candle in order that she could keep him warm and watch for any change in his situation. She sat on the bottom of the bunk, taking up as little space as she could.

Mack brought food, beer, a bucket of water, cloths and a bottle of brandy. "He could need some of that when he wakens; he took a solid beating."

"Thank you," Milly responded. "I've never seen anything like it. I don't understand how human beings can inflict such damage to each other; it's barbaric."

"It's all some people know," Mack responded quietly. "Don't eat the food all at once; it's likely I won't be back for some time."

There was no point in Milly wondering what tasks Mack had to do that took him away from her. It was nothing to do with her, and knowing would not achieve any solution to her predicament. She remained standing until the door locked behind Mack, and then she poured some water into her cup before holding it over the fire to take the chill off the water.

Using the cloths supplied, Milly wiped the dried blood from Henry's face, hands and arms. He had arrived dressed only in breeches, his shirt and boots.

She took off his boots so he would be more comfortable. Having wrapped him in the blanket, she monitored his temperature, afraid of a fever developing and worried that he had not regained consciousness.

Milly sat on the edge of the bunk, placing a cool damp cloth on Henry's forehead until it warmed up, and she replaced it with a fresh cloth. She moved his hair away from his face, trying to wash away the traces of blood that had become attached to his hair. Henry looked a little better than he had when he had been brought in, but his face was a mess.

Henry eventually moaned, and Milly shushed him, stroking his cheek gently in a soothing motion. "My lord, you are safe," she soothed.

"Miss Holland? Milly?" Henry croaked.

"Yes." Milly smiled at the use of her given name.

Henry opened his eyes, realising soon enough that he could open only one, the other being closed due to swelling. "Have they hurt you?"

"No. But they've hurt you."

"Feel bloody awful," Henry muttered.

"Here have some of this," Milly moved to lift Henry's head, so she could raise the brandy bottle to his lips.

Henry winced as the alcohol stung his cut lips but gulped the liquid, welcoming the taste and knowing the effect would numb some of the pain he was feeling. He had never felt as sore in his life. "Is this smuggled?"

he asked, trying to inject some humour into a very dark situation.

"Probably," Milly responded with a small smile. "I don't think anything here will have been gained by legitimate means."

"I think we're in a bit of a pickle, Milly. Can I call you Milly?" Henry asked, looking at her seriously.

Milly realised how bad Henry must be feeling because of the fact that he had not attempted to sit up. "I think we've moved a little beyond formalities, haven't we?"

"Yes. I'm Henry from now on. I'm glad you'll be speaking my name; your voice is always so soothing and gentle, almost like a gentle kiss. My name will sound good on your lips."

"Do you ever stop flirting?" Milly asked, but she had flushed with pleasure at his words.

"Not while there's breath in my body."

"I think you'd better conserve that breath at the moment and rest. You've been through a right old time of it and need a while to recover. Try to sleep. I know the bunk isn't the best, but it's all we've got."

Henry looked around the room as best he could. "Where will you sleep?"

"I'm going to nurse you tonight. I'll sleep in the morning when you awaken."

Henry wriggled towards the wall and turned onto his side. The movement caused him to grimace in pain, and he paused when a wave of nausea passed over him; he must have damaged his ribs if the pain was anything to go by.

"Join me; we can both fit on here," he indicated that Milly lie beside him.

"No!" Milly responded, shocked at the suggestion.

"Why not?"

"I've not washed in days."

"That doesn't worry me; I can't imagine I smell too pleasantly after spending goodness knows how long on the dockside. It's the sensible solution."

"For a rake maybe, but my reputation has received enough trials so far in my life; it would never recover from this!"

Henry looked genuinely upset before he sighed and spoke. "Milly, I don't know if I can get us out of this. I think your reputation in front of a bunch of traitorous villains is the least of our worries."

Milly paused. He was right; neither was sure that this was going to end happily; she might as well take the pleasure of being wrapped in his arms; it could be the last thing she did.

Wrapping her cloak tightly around her body, she sat on the bunk and lay down. Henry had smiled at the action; she was still being prim even though she had given way to his suggestion. He placed one arm under her neck and folded it over her body, pulling her close to him, putting his other arm around her waist. He curled his body around hers, resting his head on the pillow.

"Thank you," he whispered and kissed her hair gently. "I'm sorry you've been put through this. I will do my damndest to get you out of here, if it's the last thing I do."

"Please don't talk like that," Milly responded quietly, feeling bolder when she did not have to look at him.

"You're here because of me."

"And you're here because of me. Go to sleep."

Henry kissed her head once more and sighed into her hair. He had never felt as bad in his life, both emotionally and physically, but he would have chosen no other place to be at that moment. She fitted into him like nothing or no one had ever done before.

He closed his eyes and drifted into a surprisingly contented sleep.

*

Milly awoke lying in the same position in which she had fallen asleep. She could easily allow herself to feel happy at her position, but it was ridiculous to let her romantic ideas come to the fore in such a situation. She attempted to move slowly, but strong arms held her fast.

"Where do you think you're going?" came the gruff voice of Henry.

"I-er. To get some food," Milly stuttered.

"There's no hurry is there?" Henry truly did not want to let her go. He had suffered from a more disturbed sleep than Milly, the pain of his injuries waking him from time to time. Each time he had kissed Milly's hair and lain with his nose buried in the thick tresses, which were dishevelled by many days of being unbrushed.

"We shouldn't," Milly insisted. It would be so easy to forget her principles but, if she did, she would, as a consequence, lose her grip on her self-control, which would result in the reality of the situation taking hold. She could not afford to lose control.

Henry sighed. "Why are you so good?"

Milly chuckled at his response. "Why do you make it sound a trait to be despised?"

"When it prevents me from keeping you wrapped in my arms, it is," Henry said before kissing her head one last time.

Milly felt her mind was at odds with her heart and felt bereft when Henry removed his arms enough that she could easily move off the bunk. Her colour was heightened as she busied herself, emptying the ash out of the brazier in readiness for the next fire and dividing the remaining food in two.

"I don't know when our next meal will arrive, but there's not really enough to split it over two meals each," she explained apologetically, handing Henry the food.

"As I can barely open my mouth without it hurting, I think it will take some time to devour this small feast," Henry responded wryly.

"Would you like some brandy to help with the pain?"

"Not this early. Even I have limitations!"

Milly smiled and joined Henry on the bunk. He had sat up and, although they were not touching, they were seated far closer to each other than would have been allowable in any respectable drawing room.

"Have they mistreated you?" Henry asked, eating very slowly. He did not really want to eat, but what Milly had said was true, they should eat while they could.

"No. When I was brought here, I thought I wouldn't have been able to stand it; there was mention of rats. I couldn't have coped with being in total darkness with the sounds of rats, but Mack brought me the fire, candles and the wood for blocking the hole over there. I've heard them running in the walls, but thankfully not seen them."

"Mack?" Henry asked in disbelief.

"Yes, do you know him? He brought you in last night."

"I'll kill him!" Henry snarled.

"I don't understand," Milly said in confusion. Mack had been the kindest person she had met since her nightmare had begun; she could not understand Henry's reaction.

"The situation is worse than I thought, Milly."

Henry offered no other explanation, but the atmosphere changed. Milly sensed he was in a dark place and, although curious about the connection between the two men, she held her counsel.

Neither mentioned Mack again for the rest of the day, but the mood did not really return to the comfortable one it had been in the morning despite the circumstances.

There was one other hurdle to get over, involving using the crude petty. After a lot of negotiation, which involved Henry being amused and Milly being mortified, agreement had been reached that involved them each in turn facing the wall and sticking their fingers in their ears. Henry had increased Milly's discomfort by singing at the same time, but it had been done as an effort to give Milly the opportunity to curse Henry and relieve some of the mortification she was feeling.

Just as Milly was considering making a fire for the evening, the door opened. If Joshua had entered bringing attention to the fire would have been a disaster, although with Henry seated at her side, the thought of rats in the dark was not quite so terrifying.

Luckily, it was Mack who walked through the door, closing it firmly behind him, while trying to carry a basket of food and jug of beer.

At the sight of Mack, Henry jumped to his feet, the movement causing him to wince in pain, but the discomfort not preventing him from carrying out what he had been waiting to do all day.

"You'd better be armed because I'm going to kill you—you traitorous bastard!"

Chapter 16

Mack calmly placed the tray and jug on the table, watching Henry the whole time. "Keep your voice down, you young fool!" he snapped. "Do you want to see us all killed?"

"You, yes, definitely! There aren't words you could utter that could make this any better!"

"Well, I won't bother then."

Henry growled in frustration. "You knew I was tearing London apart to find her, yet you were the one looking after her? Which of course leads me to not unnaturally believe that when I was seeking out Shambles to stop something like this happening in the first place, you knew exactly where he was."

"I was obeying orders."

"*I* gave you orders!"

Mack smiled slightly. "We are all tiny cogs, even you; it's just the rest of us realise that. If you choose to ignore it, that's your mistake not mine. I gave you what information I could."

"Who do you answer to?"

"The same person you keep ignoring. You've angered people by being headstrong and stubborn."

"And what? Should have I left her to face her own fate?" Henry snapped, nodding at Milly, who was watching the exchange with fascination.

"You were being an idiot before then. You had to get that picture circulated didn't you?"

"Shambles was on the run."

"To lead us to a bigger prize." Mack turned to Milly. "Don't light the fire, Joshua will be here before the evening's out."

"Oh, no," Milly said quietly, looking at Henry with concern. Both men were unpredictable at the best of times; being confined in a small room with one being a prisoner was not a mixture that would end well.

Mack left the room, and Henry paced, his fists in tight balls, all pain forgotten in his anger.

Milly tried to pacify him. "We all had a part to play in this mess," she said reasonably. "I could have easily refused to draw the picture, but instead I let my vanity be stroked and gave you the tools to seek out Shambles."

"You are completely innocent in all this!" Henry growled. "I should have left you alone."

Personally, Milly was still glad he had not left her alone. Her smitten heart could not but appreciate every moment with him, no matter how ridiculous or dangerous the situation. For the thousandth time she questioned her sanity in refusing to marry the man she so clearly loved.

"I need to ask you to do something that won't come easy," Milly said when Henry had finally calmed down enough to return to sitting on the bunk.

"Oh?"

"Please don't antagonise Shambles when he comes in."

"That's a promise I won't make," Henry responded, belligerently.

Milly sighed; she knew it was a lot to ask of him. She reached out and took hold of his hand. "I wouldn't ask this normally, but please, do it for me. I can't stand the thought of him taking you away from me. Having you here has made this prison more bearable."

Henry did not respond immediately. He was not unaffected by her words which, as with everything else to do with Milly, came as a surprise to him. The thought of causing her distress felt like a lump of lead in his stomach; he could not increase her anxiety.

"I won't aggravate the situation," Henry said quietly. "But it is only for you that I do it. I have history with Shambles that one day needs to be resolved. I won't make this situation worse, though; I need to get you to safety before I tackle him."

"A history that involves more than smuggling or being a traitor to the King?"

"Yes, much more."

Milly did not press Henry when he offered no further explanation. It was his business, and he would tell her more when he was happy to do so.

*

The small portion of sky they could see was darkening before the door opened and Joshua Shambles walked in followed by Mack. Henry glared at both men but kept his word to Milly and did not say anything to Joshua.

Their captor looked delighted with the situation, a mocking smile on his damaged face. "Not so confident now, are we?"

Henry did not respond, but his fists clenched.

"Go on, take a swipe, and I'll finish off what I should have done when I had you on the floor writhing in pain," Joshua sneered.

Milly moved her hand and covered one of Henry's.

"Aw, look at the little old maid, desperate to protect her Lord. It won't do any good, you know; once I've used you both to get my pardon, I'll make sure he gets what's coming to him. One day he'll be somewhere he shouldn't, and I'll be waiting."

"Never one for doing anything open and above board are you Shambles?" Henry snapped.

"Ooo, has the little Lord been upset? I'm so sorry you don't agree with my methods but, unless you've forgotten, we're fighting a war."

"You weren't fighting a war when you lived in Ramsgate," Henry said. His promise to Milly was costing him dearly; he wanted to rip Joshua apart, or at least die trying to.

"Ramsgate? What's Ramsgate got to do with anything?" Joshua asked, looking genuinely puzzled.

"Your response shows just the type of man you are; you can't even remember what you did to her. Did she mean absolutely nothing to you?" Henry's voice was full of pain, an effect he would like to have hidden, but the feelings were too raw to conceal.

"Ramsgate?" Joshua muttered to himself and then his eyes lit up. "Of course! Lady Mabel! How could I have forgotten? She was the sweetest little thing and so smitten with me. A pity I was visited by her guardians and told to clear off."

"You were tested and failed."

"Tested? What young man wouldn't swap one thousand pounds for the pleasures of one young lady? There was a country full of sweet little virgins to explore, especially with a pocket full of blunt."

Henry dove at Joshua, his words too much for him to bear. Mack intervened and, with one swift punch, managed to knock Henry backwards, sending him reeling onto the bunk and hitting his head on the wall with a dull thud.

Milly winced but wondered if Henry would have been quite so easy to stop if he had not already taken a severe beating.

"Moves like that could get you killed," Joshua responded quite happy with the way the situation had played out.

"If I took you with me, it would be worth it."

"But if you didn't, I might just enjoy your little spinster's body before I killed her."

Henry looked to move, but Milly moved once again to place her hand on his. "I'm not worth being killed for," she said quietly.

"Let me be the judge of that," Henry said gruffly but he relaxed back on the seat. He was no fool; Joshua would not touch him when he had Mack to do the dirty work, and Mack was in a far better condition than Henry was at the moment.

"Ah, shame," Joshua sneered when it was clear that Henry was not going to respond. "We shall have to talk about Lady Mabel again soon. I wonder where she is now?"

Joshua and Mack left the room, leaving Henry and Milly staring at the closed door in silence. It was not long before Mack returned alone, his excuse: bringing another jug of beer.

When he had secured the door behind him he turned to Henry. "You might have a death wish, but think of her," he said nodding towards Milly.

"I do, regularly," Henry responded.

"You could have fooled me! Who's Lady Mabel? Some sweetheart that Joshua stole from you?" Mack snapped, at the end of his tether with the foolish Lord.

"She was my sister."

"Oh," Mack responded. "I didn't realise. What happened to her?"

"She was fifteen but had been ill, so was bundled off to Ramsgate for some sea air and recuperation. That snake discovered her and romanced her until she was besotted with him. Her guardians thought he was a fortune hunter and so offered him a thousand pounds in exchange to disappear from her life forever. I think if he'd have chosen her, they would have let them marry. Only he was as shallow as he is now and took the money."

"She was probably better off without him," Mack said, not unreasonably; he knew Joshua better than anyone.

"Not really. She was already with child but no one knew," Henry said with anguish.

"I'm sorry. It can't have been easy."

"It was to be harder. She was so ashamed that one morning she just walked into the sea and didn't stop moving out towards the open sea until it was too deep. She left a note, explaining about the baby and her shame at being taken in by him. She said that, although he didn't love her, she couldn't live without him. She couldn't swim. I don't need to go on do I?"

The room was quiet for a few moments while the occupants let Henry's words sink in.

"I'm sorry," Mack said, finally breaking the silence. "No wonder you hate him. I'm impressed you've been so restrained. I want to kill the weasel for you."

"I won't stop you," Henry said with a small smile.

"I'll return shortly," Mack said before leaving the room.

Milly had been silent throughout the exchange, but tears had sparkled in her eyes as she had listened to the story. Henry turned to her and smiled a little, his own eyes unusually bright. "It's a sad story isn't it?" he asked quietly. "I think my heart broke that day and has never worked the same since. You did right in refusing to marry me, Milly; I'm damaged goods."

Milly cupped his cheek in her hand. "You are a loving brother, nothing else."

"But I let her down!" Henry said admitting the circumstance that haunted his every day.

"How did you do that?"

"I was living it up in London; it was my first season. While I was involved in all manner of debauchery, she was having her heart broken with no one to turn too."

"I doubt she would have turned to an older brother even if you were nearby," Milly reasoned. "And you were what – seventeen? Eighteen? Hardly capable of dealing with such a situation."

"I should have been there for her."

"It isn't your fault. You had sent her to the seaside to recover. No one could have predicted that she would meet a fortune hunter. No one could have guessed that would happen in a place usually used for recuperation."

"She was preyed on by someone with far more experience than she had, than I had."

"Many are. That's how the likes of Shambles get away with what they do. Look how he preyed on

Charles; a young boy who doesn't have a wicked bone in his body. Your sister wouldn't want you to still be suffering by blaming yourself for so many years."

Henry looked anguished. "Throughout the letter, she kept apologising to me, saying how sorry she was to have let me down."

"She wouldn't want you to get killed in trying to vindicate what happened to her, and you will if you try anything while we are in here."

"I can't let him escape again. I've accepted my fate, I just need to get you to safety first. I will not have your death on my conscience, too," Henry said, touching Milly's free hand.

"I can't bear to think of you being killed," Milly said honestly.

"You're the only one who would miss me. I'm not held dear by many."

"That's because they haven't seen what I have."

"And yet you wouldn't marry me. That's not much of a recommendation is it?" Henry said, but he was smiling his teasing smile.

"I –"

The door opened and Mack returned with a roll of cloth. "I thought you a headstrong idiot. I apologise. Use these wisely and remember we need Joshua alive, or we won't find out who the traitor higher in the ranks is. That has to be top priority."

He threw the cloth at Henry who caught it deftly. Henry waited until Mack left the room before unravelling the cloth. In the middle were two knives and a small pistol.

"Thank you Mack," Henry said quietly as he checked the gun. "Milly, you are going to be returning home soon."

Chapter 17

For the next few hours Milly sat with a sick feeling in her stomach. She could not eat a morsel of the food Mack had brought; how could she eat when Henry was prepared to die in order to seek vengeance against Joshua? There was nothing she could do to change his mind; too many years had passed; the hatred was embedded too deeply for him to be able to let it go. He was determined to get her free but after that he would be careless with his life. Milly was not sure how she would be able to face a world without Henry at its centre.

Henry had put the pistol in the back of his breeches, the small size being easily concealed by his untucked shirt. One knife he tucked in the top of his boot and the other he gave to Milly.

"Just in case," he had said with a smile.

Milly always wore her cape, the damp air keeping her chilled if she just sat in her thin cotton gown. She tucked the knife in her cape pocket, not foolish enough to think that she might not need it. The outcome of the next few hours, or maybe days, was going to be unpredictable. She would have to be braver than she had ever been before. She prayed, rather than believed, they would emerge unscathed; Henry was still not strong, and she doubted his ability to fight his way out; even if they managed to leave the room, there would obviously be other men in the warehouse.

During the dark night hours, Henry lay down on the bunk. "Come and join me; we both need some rest. It's been a trying day."

Milly hesitated. "We shouldn't."

"We did last night."

"That doesn't make it right," came the prim response.

Henry laughed. "You will never fail to amuse me; come here, let a dying man have a last night cuddled up to the woman he adores."

Milly flushed but responded confidently enough. "As I'm the only woman for miles, that's not necessarily a compliment!"

Henry chuckled, but tucked Milly next to him as he had done the previous night. He knew so many other women who were more beautiful, more experienced than Milly, but there was nowhere he would rather be than curled up next to her.

Milly felt so protected wrapped in Henry's arms. She had come so close to telling him that she had made a mistake; she wanted more than anything to be married to him whether he broke her heart or not. Over the last few days she had come to realise that being with him in any form was better than being separated from him.

She had been interrupted by Mack, and the reality was he had saved her from revealing her true feelings to Henry, which would have put even more guilt on him. So much had been explained by being told the story of his sister and the burden he had carried around for so many years. She could not now declare her feelings and increase his self-recriminations for causing her to be in this situation.

Milly realised Henry could have ravished her if he had wanted too, but he had been a gentleman, apart from the odd sleeping arrangements, of course. That was more out of necessity than anything else. Although he teased her about not marrying him, perhaps he had rethought his offer. If that were the case she was even more relieved that she had been interrupted.

*

Both slept late into the following morning and were only disturbed by Mack's entrance. He nodded at them, his face not betraying any emotion at finding them curled together. Milly moved quickly off the bunk, blushing furiously at being caught in such a compromising position.

"I won't be back at all for the rest of the day," he informed them.

"Oh? Anything going on that I should be aware of?" Henry asked, stretching without a care, acting as if sleeping with Milly was the most natural thing in the world.

Mack raised his eyebrow. "Nothing to concern you."

"I doubt that, but you've shown that you have many layers Mack, so I'm not surprised at your reticence. Who'd have thought the amenable Mack would prove such a double agent."

"Mock all you like; you have no idea what it's like day to day for any of us," Mack said quietly.

"That's true, I don't," Henry acknowledged. His mocking tone had gone; Mack was doing a dangerous job, one that if caught would result in instant death.

"You stick to what you're good at, and I'll do the same," Mack said with a half-smile before leaving them alone once more.

"You shouldn't torment him; he must be in a difficult position," Milly chided.

Henry smiled. "He can give as good as he gets; he's just being restrained because you're here."

"Well, I'm glad. There aren't enough people to keep you from becoming too self-absorbed."

Henry spluttered. "Goodness! You do have a fine opinion of me!"

This time it was Milly's time to smile. "I like to think it's realistic."

"Termagant!"

Milly laughed quietly and busied herself with splitting the food into enough meals that they would stave off hunger for the day. She had not felt full since her captivity, but she was not starving; they were being provided with enough food to not starve but not enough to ever feel content after eating.

"I would love to eat something sweet." Milly, grimaced at the sight of yet another day of mainly bread and cheese.

"The food not up to your fine taste?"

"I have a sweet tooth at the best of times; now I'm positively longing for anything that is not dry and tasteless!"

"Just see it as an advantage; a sweet tooth can be a problem for a lady. An expanding waistline is often the result of too much indulgence."

"You know far too much about women," Milly said trying to be prim, her amusement showing in her sparkling eyes.

"It has been my life's work," Henry said, in mock seriousness.

"Yes, I used to think Lord Chertsey was one to watch, but in reality the outwardly more charming one was the more rakish."

Henry moved quickly, grabbing Milly around the waist and spinning her so that she was pulled against his chest. "So you think I'm charming?"

Milly had gasped, but chuckled at Henry's words. "You know you are charming."

"Yes, but I thought you considered me a wastrel."

"Well, yes, I do, but I can see your attractions just like every other female in society."

"Oh, Milly, how I wish we were exchanging these words somewhere else," Henry moaned, resting his head on her forehead.

"I think for both our sakes, it's probably a good thing we aren't."

"You torture me, woman!"

"Because I don't pander to you?"

"That and the fact that I know you'd prevent me from kissing you senseless if I tried."

Milly paused, and Henry's eyes lit up at the hesitation. "Miss Holland, I do believe you want to be kissed by me!"

"Just because I want something, doesn't mean I'm going to get it."

"Have either of us got anything to lose?" Henry's tone had turned serious.

"I have to believe so, or I believe I will lose control, and the fear of our situation will overwhelm me," Milly replied honestly.

"I'm going to do my damndest to protect you."

"I know, and I believe you, but you might not be able to. I realise we might not get out of here. Either of us."

"In that case, we should definitely be enjoying kisses." Henry bent forward and gently kissed Milly's lips; he was testing her, giving her the opportunity to stop him if she wished. Just as Henry moved to deepen the kiss, the lock in the door was released, the door opening.

"Damn it!" Henry cursed and although he moved away from Milly, he remained close to her; they were not expecting anyone so soon.

Joshua Shambles stormed into the room. "What is it about you lot?" he raged at Henry. "Why can't you keep out of business that doesn't concern you?"

Henry had instinctively moved in front of Milly and moved her so she stood closer to the door. If the situation deteriorated, she had the chance of reaching the door if he managed to delay Joshua.

"What are you talking about?" Henry drawled, every fibre ready to act at the first sign of escape.

Joshua pulled out a pistol and aimed it at Henry's chest but was prevented from responding by a commotion outside the prison cell. Everyone turned to see Lord Chertsey entering with Mack positioned in front of him, a gun pointing at the back of Mack.

"Edmund, what an absolute delight to see you," Henry said pleasantly as if they were exchanging pleasantries in Hyde Park.

"What sort of bloody mess have you been causing now, Grinstead?" Edmund said roughly. "I can't leave you alone for a few weeks and all hell breaks loose!"

"You know how tedious life can get in society. I decided it was about time this rascal was brought to heel," he said, nodding to Joshua.

"You're like a dog with a bone."

"Hopefully, now you're here, we can sort this out once and for all. Now, Shambles, are you going to come quietly, or will you require a good beating first?" Henry said good-naturedly, taking the pistol out of his pocket and pointing it in the direction of Joshua.

Chapter 18

"Now isn't this going to be interesting?" Joshua said, not at all fazed that he was out-gunned.

"Isn't it just?" Henry responded pleasantly. "I've waited a long time for this Joshua."

"Don't we know it," Edmund said, rolling his eyes a little. His stance had relaxed; this was clearly a fight between Joshua and Henry; the rest of the group were merely bystanders. His gun he rested on his arm, ready to spring into action at a second's notice if Mack should move.

Joshua looked at Henry. "You'll never get out of here alive. My men will realise there's something amiss soon. Let's see if you're so confident then, shall we?"

"I apologise for putting a dampener on the event, but I think you'll find your men are being held by mine," Edmund said. "They weren't too keen on starting a gun fight, so they gave up quite gracefully. It was a refreshing start to the evening."

"Damned cowards!" Joshua spat. He turned to Henry. "All this because I ruined your sweetheart? A little overreaction isn't it?"

Edmund raised his eyebrow in question at Henry; Mack looked resigned, while Milly stepped closer to Henry. Henry did not see Milly's movement, but Mack indicated she should not move closer; he moved her so she was standing close to himself, he did not wish Milly to be caught in the crossfire between Henry and Joshua, which he was sure was inevitable.

"She was my sister," Henry growled, his voice low.

Joshua looked genuinely surprised at the information. "Really? I obviously didn't ask the right questions when I was enjoying her flesh." He smiled when he noticed Henry's hand tighten around the pistol. "Oh, you don't like to know that your baby sister enjoyed her time with a real man?"

"Joshua…," Mack said quietly.

"What?" Joshua snapped. "I'm just telling the truth; if he can't handle that, it's not my problem."

"Have you no remorse that you killed her?" Henry said.

"Killed her? Dead is she? That's a shame; she was a pretty little thing, but it had nothing to do with me. I left her alive and well." There was not a morsel of remorse in Joshua.

"Not quite so well. She was carrying your child," Henry said.

Milly noticed the abject despair that sounded in Henry's voice, and her heart broke for him.

Joshua looked taken aback at Henry's words. "She was having my child? What happened to it? Did she die in childbirth? Where is the child now?"

"She couldn't face the world when she found out the baby was on the way. She walked into the sea and kept walking," Henry said.

"She murdered my child!" Joshua spat, all too easily falling into his pattern of blaming anyone else apart from himself.

"You murdered your child as if you had walked into the sea with her yourself!" Milly snapped, sick and tired of Joshua being able to get away with everything.

"Ah, so the spinster talks!" Joshua mocked. "You were the same when I stayed with your pathetic cousin, keen to whisper poison into everyone's ear. What would you know about it, you dried-up reject of a woman!"

"Leave her out of this; it's between you and me," Henry snarled.

"But she's just made it about herself," Joshua reasoned. He turned his gun so it aimed at Milly instead of Henry.

Milly stood perfectly still, her eyes widened in fear, but there was no other outward sign of reaction to the change in circumstances.

"Ah, damn, that changes everything," Henry said. "I'm sorry, Mack, I truly am."

"Sorry, Mack? Why are you apologising to Mack?" Joshua snapped, looking with suspicion at his henchman.

Henry spoke before Mack had any opportunity to, but Mack was watching them both closely. "You see, Mack must think more of you than I do because he didn't want me to kill you, but you made a fatal mistake. You pointed a gun at Miss Holland, and I have to take exception to that, Shambles. You just can't go around pointing guns at fine ladies."

With Henry's words, he pulled the trigger of the gun he was still pointing at Joshua.

Mack shouted "No!" and jumped towards Henry.

Edmund's gun moved from its resting place and, pointing the barrel at Mack, Edmund pulled the trigger.

Milly saw what Edmund was doing and pushed Mack with all her might, sending Mack sprawling across the floor.

All four actions seemed to happen instantaneously within a second. Those still standing looked at Joshua's body, lain prone on the floor, clearly dead having received a bullet at such short range. The last expression on his face, was that of surprise.

Henry turned to Milly and looked at her in horror. "Milly!" he moaned, seemingly unable to move to her.

"Lord Chertsey didn't know Mack was a good man. I couldn't let him shoot him, it wouldn't have been fair for all his kindnesses to me," Milly responded, colour draining from her face. She smiled slightly at Henry's worried face. "Henry, I think I've been shot."

Henry moved to catch Milly as she fainted. He had seen the blood staining her dress. He had been more frightened than at any other time in his life. She had been shot, and he did not know how to make it better.

Luckily, Edmund still had his wits about him and barked commands to Henry that he followed dumbly. Henry was ushered through the building and out into the open air. He staggered a little when hit with the brightness of the day; his eyes complaining of the sudden bright light, but he refused to give Milly up when Edmund tried to take her from him.

Mack had disappeared and neither man registered the fact or would have been concerned if they had. Edmund called for his carriage and, once it was brought round, they carefully lifted Milly into it. Henry and Edmund sat down, Henry placing Milly's head on his lap and holding her in place on the carriage seat as the equipage moved quickly through the streets.

"I'm taking her home," Henry said eventually.

"No. She's my family now; she comes to my house. Clara would never forgive me if she wasn't cared for by her."

"But she's *mine*," Henry moaned, squeezing Milly's hands.

"No she isn't, and I'm certainly not giving the care of her over to you. It's not acceptable on so many counts," Edmund said firmly. In the occupation they had been involved with, Henry had very much been leader. He was the one who liaised with the higher authority and directed Edmund on what tasks they had to work on but, in this situation, Edmund was taking charge.

He had no idea what history there now was between Milly and Henry, but she was the cousin of Edmund's wife, and therefore she was his responsibility.

They arrived at the Chertsey abode too slowly in Henry's opinion, but any faster could have hurt Milly even more. Henry had checked Milly's breathing regularly and taken a little comfort that she was breathing, although she was still unconscious.

As soon as the carriage came to a stop, Edmund jumped out and, between the two men, they lifted Milly out just as gently as they had placed her inside. Henry insisted on carrying her up the steps to the now open front door, where Clara hovered.

"My lord?" she asked Henry in horror, taking in the sight of her cousin's head lolling over Henry's arm and the deep red stain on her dress.

"She's been shot by your husband!" Henry said roughly.

"Edmund?" Clara asked, unable to comprehend what had happened from such a sentence.

"I'll explain later. The doctor is on his way; I sent someone to get him before we left the docks."

"Quickly, follow me," Clara instructed, leading the way up the stairs of the house that had only very recently become her London home.

She led the way into her own bedchamber. It was the largest in the house, apart from her husband's and would be the perfect one for nursing her cousin. She indicated that Henry place Milly on the bed.

"Leave her here until the doctor has seen her and then I'll change her into some clean clothes if she's well enough to be moved," Clara instructed.

Henry rubbed bloody hands through his hair and walked towards the window. He looked out with unseeing eyes; he had promised to keep her safe, and he had failed her just as he had failed Mabel.

Clara saw Henry's demeanour and was curious at the marked change in the Earl of Grinstead. It was something to note, but at the moment Milly was her priority.

Luckily, it was only a few minutes before the doctor arrived and was escorted to the bedchamber. Clara moved forward to greet the doctor at the same time as Edmund approached Henry.

"Come, Grinstead. Let's get you cleaned up while Miss Holland is being attended to; there's nothing we can do at the moment."

"I want to stay," Henry said quietly.

"I know, but she needs to be examined. We shall return."

Edmund led Henry through the adjoining door to his own bedchamber and dressing room. His staff had acted quickly based on what they had seen and a hot bath was already prepared in Edmund's dressing room.

"I'll leave you to bathe. My valet will sort out some replacement clothes; from the look of you I doubt those rags you are standing in will survive a wash. I need to change; there was a lot of blood," Edmund said. His tone now was more of an older brother than the commander it had been when in the warehouse.

Henry nodded, and a footman helped him with his toilette. He went through the procedure automatically without really comprehending what was happening. When he stood in front of a mirror with borrowed clothes, he saw for the first time how ghastly he looked.

Dark rings were visible under his eyes; the rest of his face was a deathly white in the gaps that were not covered with purple, black and yellow bruises. He had been shaved, but it did not make him look or feel any better.

He had felt dead inside when Mabel died. It had changed a carefree young man into a bitter being, albeit the bitterness was hidden from the rest of society. He had learned to be charming and sociable while being detached. It had enabled him to take risks because he cared about no one, especially himself. That had brought him to the attention of the people looking to persuade some members of the aristocracy that spying was not the contemptible role that it was considered.

Henry had eagerly taken on the role, the danger and deceit being attractive to someone who held society in disdain. When he had started to work with Edmund, he had appreciated the other man's equally dark outlook on life, but then Edmund had met Clara and been smitten.

Henry had thought him a fool, so it was ironic, then, that at the same time he was himself falling in love with the quiet, elegant, pretty Miss Holland.

In true Henry fashion he had put her at risk just as he had with every other person who could be useful to him. It was his just desserts that she would be taken from him in this way. He put his hands on his hips and breathed slowly in and out. He could so easily lose control at the thought of losing her.

Edmund tapped on the door of the dressing room and entered. "The doctor has spoken to me of his findings."

"And?"

"She's been very lucky. The bullet entered her body below the rib cage and passed straight through. We would find it embedded in the wall of the room if we were to go back," Edmund said, his tone positive.

"Is she conscious?" Henry asked.

"Not at the moment, but Clara said she did regain consciousness for a short time while the doctor was examining her."

"If the bullet isn't lodged inside, why is she not awake?"

"Have some sympathy! She's been shot! Whether the bullet is still there or not, she still experienced a trauma," Edmund almost laughed at Henry's unrealistic expectations.

"Thank God for your poor marksmanship," Henry said, almost able to smile.

"I will be thankful for that until my dying day," Edmund said seriously as he led the way out of the room.

Chapter 19

Milly's bloodstained clothes had been removed, and she was now lying under the covers dressed in one of her cousin's nightgowns. She had been cleaned as much as was possible on a bed, Clara being concerned at the level of grime that was attached to Milly's body.

Henry stood at the bottom of the bed. "She looks so small."

"Yes, but she has a strong constitution," Clara said gently.

"Maybe, but she's had a hard time of it recently," Henry responded, remembering their conversation about sweet items.

"The doctor is afraid of a fever, but the bullet wound itself shouldn't cause any long-lasting damage."

"Can I stay?" Henry asked, all bravado gone.

"She will be looked after well," Clara said gently. The sick room was not the place for a man; they had little patience when so confined.

"She looked after me. I promised I'd look after her. I've not done a very good job of it so far," Henry said, his eyes never leaving Milly's sleeping form.

"I will care for her. She is very dear to me," Clara said softly.

"And to me."

*

Henry was eventually persuaded against his will to leave the house and return home. He had not told Milly's family of what had gone on between them in Farnham or that Milly had intended taking up a position of companion in Ireland–something he presumed she had missed the opportunity of securing by the amount of time that had passed since they had spoken of it. It was not for him to divulge her secrets.

Sitting in his study, he drank one glass of wine after another, trying to deaden his feelings, but no amount of alcohol seemed to work.

He looked up in surprise when the study door opened; he had expressly instructed that he was not to be disturbed under any circumstances; he groaned to see Mack's form appear, closing the door behind him.

"I'd thought you'd be long gone by now," Henry muttered.

"I've two reasons for stopping by," Mack said, sitting without invitation.

"Go on, surprise me!"

"I wanted to find out how the Miss was," Mack said. He had become found of the young woman, admiring her stoic spirit.

"Alive, but not conscious."

"I owe her my life," Mack said seriously.

"You and me both in our different ways," Henry acknowledged.

"I hope she recovers soon."

"As do I."

"I thought there was something between you."

"If you could call refusing my marriage proposal something between us, I suppose you're right," Henry said with a shrug.

Mack smiled. "So, you've met someone brave enough to stand up to you. She'd be perfect for you; too many society misses would pander to your arrogance."

"Thank you for that shining recommendation," Henry said drily. "Now what was the other reason you wanted to speak to me?"

"I've been ordered to visit," Mack said looking a little uncomfortable.

"Go on."

"You've upset quite a few people in killing Joshua."

"Forgive me if I couldn't give a damn."

"They could. I've been told to tell you that your services are no longer required. If you try to interfere with the work of the Office, they'll come down on you hard."

"Is that a threat, Mack?" Henry asked, with an expression of incredulity.

"I think it will be if you don't walk away quietly," Mack replied honestly. He was not about to explain the language that had been used when he had reported the day's events to the men in the Home Office. Henry had been cursed to hell and back. Some were keen to have him made an example of but, for not for the first time, his title gave him protection. Getting rid of a peer would give the opportunity of those wanting a revolution the chance to claim his death as a victory against the establishment.

"I'd like you to take a message back from me," Henry said angrily.

"Is that wise?"

"Probably not, but as usual I don't care," Henry responded with derision. "I have written down everything that I have been involved with over the years. Every operation I have known anything about, I have made notes on. So every moment of my work, I have recorded. I often wondered what would happen if I did something they didn't like; I never considered it would be the death of Shambles. Why they don't realise I've done the country a good deed, I'll never know."

"You were told he was important," Mack said reasonably.

"And they should understand that sometimes they can't control everything. I've lodged my memoirs with someone and, before they think of paying a visit to my solicitor or Lord Chertsey, I'm not so predictable. If anything happens to me, any of my future family members or Miss Holland, for as long as she has breath in her body, those memoirs will be published in full in so many printing houses that it would be impossible to prevent at least some copies getting out. Once they're out in the public domain, I don't need to stress that there would be backlash as a result, particularly from the highest levels of our society. I'm sure some of our Dukes and Duchesses would be greatly annoyed to find how they've been manipulated and used."

"I didn't think you'd accept their threat without having something to say about it. You've planned well." Mack knew Henry's faults, but he liked the young Earl, he had spirit.

"I'm no fool, and I dislike being considered as one. They underestimate who they work with," Henry responded. His argument was not with Mack, especially as in some ways he had looked after Milly. Henry was realistic enough to accept that Milly's spell in her prison could have been a lot worse.

"They won't risk exposure."

"If they leave me alone, I'll leave them alone. There is nothing else to say; they'll be glad to see the back of me, and I'm not sorry to see that chapter closed."

Mack stood. "I wish you well even though you've made my job harder. I do understand why you wanted to kill Shambles; I didn't at the start."

"I knew I was going to kill him a long time before I joined the Home Office," Henry said. "They just gave me the opportunity to have resources to target him."

"Yes, something which hasn't escaped their notice," Mack said with a small smile. "Goodbye, Grinstead; I hope your lady recovers."

"Good luck, Mack," Henry said, standing and shaking the offered hand. He watched Mack leave the room before refilling his glass. He had no doubt that Mack would find out who was leading the opposition in support of the French; the man had a way of getting to the heart of the matter.

Henry sighed and sat at his desk. He had not written what he had said, but he was going to have to now. Just in case those in the Home Office did not take him seriously, he had to protect his family, his future family if he could ever persuade Milly to marry him.

He started to write; it was going to be a long night.

*

Clara had stayed by Milly's bedside for most of the three days she had been in a fever. They had tried everything; bleeding, cooling, and lots of laudanum. Milly had hardly responded to anything. Her wound was a fiery red, the skin hot to the touch. Clara had refrained from writing to Mrs Holland; she was fully aware of the relationship that Milly shared with her mother and, if pushed, Clara would have admitted that she could not face dealing with her aunt whilst her cousin was so sick.

She had sent a note each morning to Henry. She had read the note he had sent to Edmund before trying to find Milly; it showed a man who was desperate to find a woman for whom he cared deeply. Each day Henry sent fresh flowers and some form of sweet treat but did not appear at the house himself.

Clara wondered, now the danger had been removed that had linked Henry and Milly together, whether he was losing interest. So it was with curiosity that she descended the stairs on the fourth day when she was told that Henry had arrived and asked to see her.

He was waiting in the small morning room, standing at the window, looking anything but relaxed.

"Good afternoon, my lord," Clara said pleasantly, crossing the room before curtseying to Henry's bow.

"Good afternoon, my lady," Henry responded.

The greeting gave Clara enough of an opportunity to take in Henry's appearance. He was looking decidedly ill, his eyes almost sunken, his skin colour looking sallow.

"Miss Holland?" Henry asked.

"The same, I'm afraid. The doctor is suggesting moving her to some sort of nursing home if she doesn't regain consciousness soon," Clara explained.

Henry seemed to sag at the words. "I'm losing her all over again."

"I don't understand."

Henry sighed; there was no longer the wish to keep his personal life away from those around him; the last few days had been hell. He was in no fit state to play games with words, which had once been his forte.

"I'd asked her to marry me when I visited her in Farnham. I saw how things were with that buffoon who'd thrown her over when there was no money forthcoming; added to that, he caught us kissing; so I proposed to your cousin."

"She never wrote to me about it," Clara responded in some surprise.

"No, she must have decided it wasn't important enough; you see, she turned me down. She was intent on throwing her life away on some position as a companion in Ireland! I couldn't talk her out of it; neither could her friend; she was as bloody minded as I am!"

Clara suppressed the smile at Henry's words; she could see he was not ready to see humour in any situation at the moment. "Go on."

"But in the days in the cell, I thought she had feelings for me. I thought she'd been more inclined to consider me an eligible match, but it seems I am losing her again."

"I presumed that once you'd returned home, you would forget about what had gone on. I had seen that you had some feeling for her when you first returned her home. I assumed it had worn off by now," Clara said honestly.

"Do you think I'm so callous? I suppose my previous behaviour has not had anything in it to recommend it, so I can see you would have believed me to be capable of that."

"I'm sorry if it seems harsh."

"You've nothing to be sorry about. For years, I've had a lump of ice where everyone else has a heart. Your low opinion of me is well deserved," Henry acknowledged.

"My cousin is a far better judge of character than I am," Clara acknowledged. "She knew that there was something amiss with Lord Chertsey, while I was smitten," she said with a small smile. "She was also quick to notice the change in him. If she had feelings for you, I'm convinced you deserved her regard."

"Can I see her?"

"Nothing has changed since your last visit," Clara said gently.

"I need to see her. I feel as if I'm actually fading away without having her near me. Does it make sense to say even though we were locked away, I enjoyed my time with her?" Henry tried to explain.

Clara realised that this usually confident man had fallen deeply in love with her cousin. She was not convinced he realised what had happened to him, but she was sure it *had* happened. Her heart ached for his suffering, which would only increase if Milly did not recover. She made a decision; she would not be the one to keep them apart.

"Follow me, My Lord. You are welcome to stay with Milly for as long as you wish."

Chapter 20

There was a change in Milly; Henry saw it immediately. She looked far more fragile than she had on that first day. Her skin was almost translucent. He could have wailed at the sight of her; if he had held any hope that she might recover, it had been dashed the moment he entered the room.

Clara saw the pain in Henry's eyes and gently touched his arm. "Sit with her; talk to her. I will leave you alone, but ring the bell if you need any help at all. You won't be disturbed otherwise."

Henry nodded unable to speak and only after the door had closed behind Clara, did he move to the side of the bed. Sitting on a vacant seat, he pulled back the bed cover and reached for Milly's hand. It was stone cold.

Henry moved to sit on the edge of the bed and started to gently rub the hand to warm it. Clara had said that Milly had a fever, but she was so cold he didn't understand how she could be feverish. But if she was not, he had no idea what was wrong.

Rubbing and massaging the skin, he started to talk quietly, feeling foolish at first, but his need to make her better drove him on.

"Now then, Miss Holland, I expected you to be running around by now," he started. "Causing all this fuss over a little gunshot. I never had you down for one who enjoyed the dramatics. Goodness knows what your future employer will think of this lax behaviour."

Henry paused, to swap hands, tucking the now slightly warmer limb back under the covers. "I thought of writing to your friend and asking her to contact your employer and explain what had happened, but then I remembered that I hadn't wanted you to go, so why should I help your cause? I want you to stay with me, Milly; never forget that."

Henry kept talking until his mouth was dry and he had run out of words. He looked at the still figure and made a decision. "Milly, if you object, now is the time to raise it otherwise I shall take your silence as agreement. You see, my sweetheart, I've missed you so much these last few days, and I need to be close to you."

He discarded his frock coat and waistcoat and took off his boots. Climbing under the covers with her, he tried to hold her as he had when they had slept together in the prison. Since returning home he had not had a good night's sleep, unable to find comfort without the feel of his Milly by his side. Moving her was done slowly and with care until Henry was wrapped around her body once more, protecting her and comforting himself.

He lay his head on her hair and kissed her head gently. "Come back to me, Milly. Please don't leave me; life is too bleak without you by my side."

*

There was a sound that she could not place,– a noise that was disturbing yet comforting at the same time. She tried to ignore it, but it would not go away. In a way she longed for it; at the same time she wanted to swipe her hand to rid herself of the nuisance.

Everything was black and hot. It had been so hot for such a long time now that she no longer fought against it; it was easier to let it wash over her. The thought of the blackness was no longer frightening; until the buzzing started she had been content to let the darkness take her for good. Now though, now it seemed oppressive.

The buzzing eventually stopped, but pain ripped through her body. She had no idea what was happening, only that it hurt. The pain soon passed though, and she felt safe again and comfortable; she had not felt comfortable in the blackness; it had just been easier to stay there than to fight it.

Something had changed. It almost felt as if she was rising to the surface of some weighty substance that had been pushing her down. Now though, she was being drawn upwards, only she was not sure if she had the strength to reach the top, wherever that was.

Milly slowly opened her eyes, her lids feeling unnaturally heavy. At first she thought there was just more blackness, but after blinking her eyes and focusing, she saw that she was in a bed in the dead of night. The fire in the grate opposite the bed was very low, hardly casting any light into the room. It must be hours since the fire was last attended to.

It seemed right to be wrapped in Henry's arms. She had known they were his arms even before she opened her eyes. No one or anything else had ever made her feel so secure, so completely embraced than when she had been in Henry's arms.

She sighed as her eyes continued to move around the room. It was a strange room; she had no idea where she was but, as long as Henry was by her side, nothing else mattered.

Drifting back into sleep, she was determined that the next time she woke, she would touch his arms.

Henry awoke with a start. There had been a change. He wondered if someone had come into the room, but he could detect no movement. Clara had been true to her word by not disturbing him, only sending a maid to deliver food and restock the fire. The maid had not reacted to see the visitor lying on the bed, only partially dressed; she was either very experienced or very discreet.

No, no one had entered the room since then. He listened to try to work out what had disturbed his slumber. After a moment, the realization of what had changed made him smile, something he had not done in days. Her breathing was deeper, not the shallower gasping breath it had been when he had first arrived, but the deeper, more healthy sound of someone in a contented slumber.

Something had happened; whether the fever had broken, he had no idea, and he did not care. She was more stable, of that he was sure, and he would do everything in his power to help with her recovery.

Closing his eyes, Henry slipped back into sleep, more content with the knowledge that somehow she was coming back to him. The smile on his face did not fade even when he was overcome with the heavier breaths of deep sleep.

Milly awoke once more. This time it was movement rather than sound that had disturbed her. Henry was moving away from her; he was trying to slide his arms from under her without disturbing her.

"No," she moaned, but it came out as nothing more than a croak, her throat was so parched.

Henry stopped as soon as he heard the noise. "Milly?" he whispered, afraid he had misheard.

Milly moved her hand. Everything took so much effort that the movement was slow and laborious, but Henry waited, unmoving to see what she did. What felt like an eternity passed before Milly finally reached his arm, and she squeezed the limb. "Don't go," she croaked.

Henry smiled and kissed her head. "Welcome back, my darling darling girl. I'm only moving to ring for some refreshment and to wash myself. I don't want to face you not looking my best. You might think I've lost my handsome features."

Milly's lips turned up in a small smile, but she did not try to stop Henry when he started to slowly move again. He was talking to her all the time, kissing her head between words. She closed her eyes, content that he would stay near.

When Henry reached the fireside, he almost pulled the rope off its mechanism he pulled it so hard. He realised it might have given the wrong impression when he heard the thud of footsteps running up the stairs. Clara was first through the door, followed closely by the maid and housekeeper.

Henry held his hand up to stop any outburst and indicated that they should leave the room. He followed them and, although he left the door slightly open, he pulled it to. "She's conscious," he said, surprising himself when tears sprang into his eyes when he uttered the words.

"Thank God!" Clara said, herself looking fit to collapse with relief.

"I want to stay with her. She didn't want me to leave her, and I promised I would return soon. I just need to freshen up, and then I'll rejoin her."

"Use my dressing room," Clara said, immediately becoming practical. She turned to the housekeeper. "Mrs Bates, we need water for his lordship and a change of shirt from my husband's wardrobe. We need food and drink, include a little for

Milly; I'm sure she won't take much, if anything, but we can always hope."

Orders despatched, she led Henry into the bedchamber and through to the dressing room. They both looked at Milly as they passed the bed, but there was no sign she was awake.

"I'll sit with her until you have finished your ablutions," Clara said. "Take your time."

"There's no chance of that. Every moment away from her is a moment wasted," Henry said before closing the door on his hostess.

Clara walked over to the sleeping Milly and gently touched her hand. It felt warmer than it had the previous day, but it was not too warm. For the first time since Milly had been brought to the house, Clara felt a normal temperature.

Milly moved slightly at the touch. "Henry?" she croaked.

Clara leaned over and kissed her cousin's forehead. "No, it's Clara, but Henry will be here soon, my sweet. He's not gone far. I am so glad to hear your voice again, Milly. We were so worried about you."

"Sorry."

"It wasn't your fault. Henry and Edmund said you were so brave, saving that man," Clara said, gently pushing Milly's hair away from her face. She would give up the role of nurse to Henry; it was clear he had done something that had brought Milly back to them, for which she would be eternally grateful but, for now, she needed to be in physical contact with her cousin; it was almost as if she did not quite believe that Milly had come back to them. "I can't imagine how frightening it was in those days in that prison."

"Henry saved me," Milly licked her cracked lips, trying to get moisture on them to make her voice clearer.

Clara put a damp cloth against Milly's lips, so she could have a few drops of liquid; she did not wish to overwhelm Milly's stomach after days of having nothing at all. "It seemed he's done it twice then, as I'm convinced his being here helped bring you back to us."

"Back to him," Milly said quietly with a little smile.

Clara squeezed Milly's hand. "I understand."

Henry entered the bedchamber feeling slightly fresher. He would have liked to have a shave, but a lady's dressing room had no equipment, so his stubble would have to wait. Leaving his braces hanging at his waist, he walked to the bed. "How's the patient?"

"Drifting in and out of sleep. She seems very tired," Clara responded.

"She's had a hard time of it. I'll get something to eat; my own appetite is finally returning; I've hardly eaten for days."

Henry tucked into the feast set out on a small table in front of the chaise longue. When he had eaten his fill he made some of the softer food into a mush type substance and poured some beer into a cup. He brought the bowl and cup round to the side of the bed.

"When she wakes I'm going to try to and get her to eat and drink something."

"Good. I'll leave you once more, but I don't want Milly thinking it isn't because I don't care. There is nowhere I would rather be than by her side, but I know she wants you here."

Henry smiled. "Thank you. I don't want to be anywhere else."

Clara left the room, and Henry sat on the chair next to the bed. He wanted nothing more than to clamber onto the covers and gather Milly in his arms again, but he could not be so selfish. She had to be cared for properly, and he was going to make sure she had everything she needed.

Milly's eyes fluttered, and she was reassured to see Henry close by. She was going to return to sleep, but he touched her arm gently.

"Do you think you could drink something?"

"No. Sleep," she croaked.

Henry smiled, "I never had you down as disobedient. I need you to try to drink something; your body needs sustenance."

Milly was lifted gently so her head was propped on Henry's arm while he fed her small amounts of the beer. When she could take no more she lay her head to the side, nestling into his shoulder.

"Milly, it is going to be difficult to get anything done when you are like this; all I want to do is stay in bed with you."

Milly smiled slightly, her eyes already closing in sleep. "Stay in bed," she whispered.

Henry kissed her head. "Of course, whatever you want, my darling."

Chapter 21

Edmund found Clara in the drawing room writing a letter. She put down the quill when her husband entered and turned to greet him. "Lord Grinstead is hoping to persuade Milly to eat and drink something. He is turning into the perfect nurse!"

Edmund looked a little concerned. "Until he loses interest. I've seen it happen before, although not under quite the same circumstances."

"Don't be so harsh! He seems to dote on her."

"Remember the Henry we knew before all this? He wouldn't be seen within ten miles of a sick bed. He probably feels guilty that he involved your cousin in his irresponsible schemes," Edmund responded, believing the cold, hard Henry to never be far from the surface. He had seen Henry turn on the charm when needed; he presumed one of those occasions was happening here.

"He should feel guilty. He was wrong to involve her, but it does seem as if he's making amends. I truly believe his being beside her helped her regain consciousness."

"That says more about your cousin's feelings than Grinstead's," Edmund pointed out.

"The only way to prove it to you is to show you what he is like with her. We'll visit tonight. I did promise to leave them alone today; I don't think constant comings and goings would do Milly any good."

*

Edmund walked into his wife's bedchamber and paused mid-stride. Henry was sitting on the side of the bed near the window, a pillow on his lap. Milly had her head resting on the pillow while Henry gently brushed Milly's hair.

Henry looked up and indicated that Edmund and Clara should remain silent. He gently removed himself from underneath Milly and, kissing her head, he moved away. He probably should not be so openly affectionate in front of everyone, but he really did not care what anyone else thought.

"How is she?" Clara whispered when Henry approached them.

"Falling in and out of sleep constantly. She has eaten something and continues to drink, so I'm happy about her progress. I'd like you to take a look at her wound. When I first arrived, you told me it was angry and swollen; I think check it before sending for the doctor unnecessarily, if it is improving, we'll just continue with what we are doing at the moment."

"If you both leave me, I shall have a look," Clara said, moving over to Milly.

Henry and Edmund left the bedchamber softly closing the door behind them.

"I never had you for a nurse," Edmund opened the conversation.

"Nor I," Henry admitted.

"When do you intend leaving us?"

"Do you wish me to leave? Are you still upset with me about what happened in Dorset?" Henry asked, a little surprised. Edmund had been as angry as he had ever seen him when he thought Clara was in danger, but that time had passed and was never going to occur again.

"No! Although I will curse you for it until my dying day," Edmund admitted. "I just presumed you would be wishing to return to the social whirl that is your life."

Henry's expression was unreadable, but he glanced at the door as if he could see through the wood into the bedroom beyond. "I'd like to stay, if it's all the same to you."

"Don't give her false hope. It wouldn't be fair."

"I think you'll find it's the other way around."

"How so?" Edmund asked in surprise at the words.

"I'm the fool who asked her to marry me, and she turned me down."

"I'm only a little surprised at that; I always thought Miss Holland was no one's fool."

"Thanks for the glowing recommendation," Henry said drily. "I'm almost glad she's incapacitated;

that way she can't send me away, and I can delay the inevitability of never seeing her again."

"Only you could find a positive in a life and death situation!"

"You know what I mean. I'm fully aware that I'm a besotted fool just as you are."

"What are you going to do?"

"I'm going to stay here, with your consent obviously, for as long as she'll have me."

"Is it your intent to wear down her defences? I'd have to object if that's your plan; the poor woman has been through enough. She doesn't deserve the onslaught of Grinstead charm that I've been unfortunate enough to witness in the past."

"No one else has ever complained."

"I don't think they realised what had hit them until you'd moved on to your next victim," Edmund responded, enjoying actually having the upper hand with Henry for once.

Henry smiled. "Everything's different now."

"Until you tire of her."

"She said something similar once, and I believed at that time it was true, but even then I'm not sure how much was just my automatic reaction to life. The thought of being faithful and loving to one person was beyond my comprehension, but that woman in there has done something to me, and I don't think I'll ever recover if I can't persuade her to marry me."

"Don't put her under any pressure," Edmund warned.

"I won't. My own pride won't let me do that. If she is to marry me, it will be because she wants to, not because I want her to. I promise you that."

Edmund inclined his head to show he was reassured. Clara came out of the bedchamber preventing any further private conversation between the pair.

"How is she?" Edmund asked.

"Her wound is not as red or swollen as it was. It was leaking puss until yesterday, but now it has closed, and she is not is in as much pain when that area is touched. I think we can leave the doctor for now."

"Is she awake?" Henry asked, already opening the door.

"Yes," Clara responded and smiled at her husband. "He didn't hear me at all, then, did he?"

"No. I think the great Lord Grinstead has actually been brought to his knees by your cousin."

"I would expect nothing else. He'd better treasure her because only the best will do for my sweet Milly," Clara said with feeling, linking her arm through her husband's as they headed to their shared bedchamber.

*

It was a week before anything like Milly's former strength returned and, even then, only partially. Henry had been persuaded to send home for the personal items he needed, although he refused the use of the room made available for him, still insisting on curling around her every night and sleeping in what was now an inappropriate situation.

Henry certainly was not going to change the situation unless forced to, and Clara and Edmund did not wish Milly to suffer a relapse. She seemed so reliant on Henry that they worried about the time when the pair were parted, which seemed inevitable at some point.

One morning before they were disturbed by the maid coming in to light the fire, Henry was still holding Milly, and he raised the subject of what had happened.

"You shouldn't have stepped in to save Mack," he gently chided, lessening the tone of the words by kissing her head.

"I couldn't let him be killed; he had been so good to me in the circumstances. It wasn't so bad in the first place I was held, but that second room," Milly shuddered. "I couldn't have borne it without Mack's help."

"He knew the risks; you could've been killed."

"But I wasn't."

"Thank God," Henry muttered into her hair. "I don't know what I would've done if you had."

Milly kissed the arm that was encircling her. "I'm here and well."

"I know."

"What do you feel about Joshua now?" It was the first time his name had been mentioned since the fateful day.

"Because of what happened to you, I didn't consider the implications for a few days. When it sank in though, it just felt as if a weight had been lifted off my shoulders. All those years trying to deliver what he deserved, and it finally happened."

"You did kill a man."

"I know and when I die I will face whatever retribution is dealt out, but for now I can only think that he got what he deserved. He had no remorse about what he had done to her or anyone else. Goodness knows how many lives he destroyed as he went through life without a conscience.

"A bit like you and your spying?" Milly asked. She was fully aware of how Henry had used people.

Henry paused. There were similarities between himself and Joshua, and he did not like to reflect on it. "I've done things I'm no longer proud of, but the difference is that I was doing most things for King and country, and revenging Mabel of course." Henry sighed into Milly's hair. "I hope I'm a better man than he is, but I'm not the one to be the judge of that."

"You are," Milly reassured him. "The way you helped me when we were confined, I will never forget."

"You are a strong person, Milly. You were coping well without me, Mack told me that."

"Maybe, but more so when you are nearby."

Milly was feeling stronger physically, but mentally her thoughts ranged from completely content when she was wrapped in Henry's embrace to desolate when she considered leaving Edmund's house, and she knew that she had to.

One morning when Henry returned to the bedchamber, he was surprised to see Milly sitting at the small Davenport desk that was in the bay window overlooking the square in the street.

"What's this?" Henry asked, walking over to the desk and gently rubbing Milly's back. That was the type of thing that Milly would miss the most; he seemed to need to be in actual contact with her, and she loved it.

"I'm finally writing to my mother," she explained. "Clara explained that she didn't want to worry mother unnecessarily, so she has not as yet informed Mother of what happened. I'm not going to tell her everything, just enough to explain why I haven't yet secured a position and, hopefully, she will allow me to stay until I'm well enough to continue my search. Even I'm not foolish enough to start employment now; I would be returning to my sick bed before the week was out."

"That's the best decision you've made in a long time," Henry responded, but his voice was empty of emotion. The thought of her leaving was like no other sensation he had ever felt, a mixture between panic and desolation.

Milly smiled slightly. "You've just seen me at my worse; I'm known for being sensible and pragmatic."

Henry moved away and sat on the chaise longue. "Do you intend to contact the lady you were meeting in Guildford?"

"No, I think I will send a letter of apology, but I doubt she would be willing to give me a second chance; I must seem very flighty."

"Everyone deserves a second chance to prove themselves."

Milly's heart sank; he was encouraging her to go to Ireland. She had missed the chance to have him in her life forever and, although he would have tired of her and had mistresses, at least she would have been able to see him every day. The thought of never being in contact with him almost made her relapse.

"Are you so keen to see me in Ireland?" she said, trying to sound light-hearted yet sounding anything but.

Henry paused. If he revealed himself, he risked a further rejection, and they had been so close these last weeks. But he could not let her leave him without saying something. For once, he had to gamble and face the possibility of rejection.

"If you do go to Ireland, you need to be aware of something."

"Oh?"

"I will be close behind, Milly. I couldn't stay in England if you were so far away from me," Henry said quietly, his usual confidence deserting him.

"You'd follow me?" Milly's heart had begun to pound at the words; she was not sure she understood their meaning.

"I would. On every afternoon off, I would be there to take you out, to court you if you gave me the slightest indication that I could ever be the man for you."

"Oh!"

"Is that all? I know you refused me and, in some respects, I understand why, but you see, Milly, so much has changed between us."

"Please don't feel guilty about what happened. You could never have predicted what would happen by asking me to draw the picture," Milly said quickly.

"Feel guilty? Yes, I do feel guilty for putting you in such a dangerous position, for leaving you alone while I stewed in a temper because you had said no. But that isn't why I'm speaking now. I can understand why you refused me; I was a wastrel, a cad who would've hurt you."

"That was only a few weeks ago," Milly said reasonably.

"Yes, and I would never have believed that so much change could happen in such a short time. Milly these past few weeks have shown me what's important, what type of man I want to be, which woman I want to be with."

Henry crossed over to Milly and crouched before her, holding her hands in his. "Milly, please give me a second chance. I can't promise to be the perfect husband; I'm a fool who's only learning how to be worthy. I'm bound to make mistakes, we both know I will. But I promise you this: I have never felt like this before, and I want to cherish the feelings and watch them grow. I cannot look at anyone else because you are my ideal."

"Don't say things that aren't true!" Milly said, a little distressed. "I don't want false flattery."

"My darling girl, it isn't! I promise you. How could it be? You're beautiful to me; you deal with everything in a quiet, confident way; you dealt with the worst of life with dignity and calmness. I want you by my side, facing everything this life throws at me, knowing that I have your love and commitment."

"Love?"

"If you don't love me, I understand. I know this is sudden, but maybe one day you will come to love me as much as I love you. You're the only person I have ever loved Milly and, even though this life has no guarantees, I know you will be the only one I ever love. I didn't know that when I first asked you to marry me, but I know it now."

Milly's eyes sparkled at the words. She cursed herself; what was it that he made her want to cry? She smiled, it was because her feelings had never been so intense about someone before. She wanted to cry because she had never felt such happiness since she had meeting him. It was time to be truthful and to a chance on him.

"Love you? Of course I love you! I loved you when you first proposed! That's why I refused you. I couldn't bear to be hurt when you turned to someone else, and I was sure you would."

"Oh, my sweet. I nearly missed the most wonderful thing to have ever happened to me! Please tell me that you trust me now not to hurt you like that?"

Milly smiled, a tear sneaking out of her crinkled eye and moving slowly down her cheek. "I do trust you, but you were so caring when you nursed me that I thought, if you'd have truly wanted me, you would have kissed me as we've kissed before."

Henry laughed and gently wiped the tear away. "It is exactly because my feelings are so deep that I haven't behaved inappropriately. For the first time in my life, I want to do the right thing. I realise that these past days would send shockwaves through society if it were known how we've been behaving, but I've needed to feel close to you. I can't sleep well unless you are in my arms, but I promise you this: I will not ruin you or compromise you in any way before we are married; that is, if you will agree to be my Lady Grinstead?"

Milly smiled. "I will. I cannot be without you, but there's just one thing."

"Anything."

"Can we please get a special licence? I don't think I can restrain myself for months."

Henry roared with laughter, wrapping his darling girl in his arms and kissing the top of her head. "Special licence it is then."

Epilogue

Lord and Lady Grinstead were soon to be known as one of the most loving couples that anyone was likely to meet in society. They were never apart, never tired of being close to each other and openly touched each other's hands, arms and on occasion even kissing when at one of the many entertainments that Lord Grinstead insisted on taking his wife to in order to show her off.

Milly had never been happier but worried that she would be too old to have children, so when they realised she was increasing, Henry decided that they were moving to their country house in order to provide the environment that was best suited to a successful birth and confinement.

The couple were eventually blessed with three young children, all girls, with which Henry was delighted. Milly despaired that her husband completely indulged their girls and was thankful that they had her nature, preventing them from being spoiled by their doting Papa.

They were joined very often by Mr and Mrs Hastings and all their brood, in the end a family with twelve children. The house was always full of noise on the extended visits that the close friends were persuaded to take.

Mrs Holland was offered a cottage on the Grinstead estate, but surprisingly turned it down. She had found a new lease of life when she could visit many in the town of Farnham, talking with pride about her daughter and her wonderful life. She particularly enjoyed visiting the Connors.

Clara and Edmund had six children, four boys and two girls who spent much of their childhood, toing-and-froing between their own home and that of their Grinstead cousins. Edmund and Henry developed a deep bond that was cemented by their love of their spouses, but would always ridicule the other, refusing to change the way they verbally spared.

Henry took Milly to visit Mabel's grave, and the pair felt able to let Mabel rest in peace now that Joshua had been punished. Henry would never quite put all the guilt to one side about what had happened to his sister, but in later years his daughters were to find that he scrutinised every gentleman that danced with them, desperate that he would not make the same mistake twice. The girls would complain, but Milly would be the peacemaker explaining time and again why their father was a trifle overprotective.

Mack did find out who was the traitor in the *ton* and one well-known family was exiled with properties confiscated. Not one to return to a normal world, Mack continued to work for the Home Office until Napoleon was defeated and there was no longer any threat of an invasion by the French.

The Home Office did leave Henry alone, but they worked on to increase the safety of the country, and eventually the role of spy became a more appealing role for the higher classes of society.

Milly had never been happier. She had never thought that falling in love with the complicated Henry would bring her such joy. If ever she woke in the night, after having a dream where she was in a dark room feeling lost, she would wake to the arms of her one true love wrapped completely around her and, sensing her upset, Henry would kiss her head, stroking her body until she fell into a more restful sleep. They never spent a night apart no matter where they were, both unable to sleep contentedly without being entwined with the love of their lives.

The End.

About this book.

These next few paragraphs might be quite controversial, but please bear with me!

I'm sure like me, you've read lots of Regency Romances where the hero is both an aristocrat and a spy. This is actually historically incorrect and, as my readers do take me to task when I get things factually wrong, I thought I'd write a spy story that was slightly different.

Spying as an occupation was not honourable in Regency England. Forget the recent television programmes and books, spying involved lying and cheating and would not have been looked on with anything but disgust by the aristocracy. Also, spying takes time. The aristocracy had to run large estates, they had involvement in the local lives of their tenants as well as being involved in London (Brighton or Bath) life: they hunted, attended the Season and don't forget the politics they were involved in! I'm not saying their lives were hard, but they were certainly full. Read any realistic spy book, and it will go into detail about the excessively large amounts of time spent watching, observing and listening. It certainly isn't something that you could dip in and out of.

That said, there is always an exception to the rule! So, I decided to give my two Earls a rebellious streak and have them involved in spying. I thought it was important that, when Clara found out what they did, she would show some of the disgust that they would have experienced if their occupation had been known by wider society.

So, I hope you've enjoyed my slight twist.

About the Author

I have had the fortune to live a dream. I've always wanted to write, but life got in the way as it so often does until a few years ago. Then a change in circumstance enabled me to do what I loved: sit down to write. Now writing has taken over my life, holidays being based around research, so much so that no matter where we go, my long-suffering husband says 'And what connection to the Regency period has this building/town/garden got?'

That dream became a little more dreamlike when in 2018, I became an Amazon StorytellerUK Finalist with Lord Livesey's Bluestocking. A Regency Romance in the top five of an all-genre competition! It was truly surreal, I didn't expect to win, but I had a ball at the awards ceremony.

I do appreciate it when readers get in touch, especially if they love the characters as much as I do. Those first few weeks after release is a trying time; I desperately want everyone to love my characters that take months and months of work to bring to life.

If you enjoy the books please would you take the time to write a review on Amazon? Reviews are vital for an author who is just starting out, although I admit to bad ones being crushing. Selfishly I want readers to love my stories!

I can be contacted for any comments you may have, via my website:

    www.audreyharrison.co.uk
    or
    www.facebook.com/AudreyHarrisonAuthor

Please sign-up for email/newsletter – only sent out when there is something to say!

www.audreyharrison.co.uk

You'll receive a free copy of The Unwilling Earl in mobi format for signing-up as a thank you!

Novels by Audrey Harrison

Regency Romances – newest release first

Lady Edith's Lonely Heart – The Lonely Hearts Series – book 1

https://www.amazon.com/dp/B0852RMGJJ

https://www.amazon.co.uk/dp/B0852RMGJJ

Miss King's Rescue – The Lonely Hearts Series – book 2

https://www.amazon.com/dp/B08778RJQP

https://www.amazon.co.uk/dp/B08778RJQP

Captain Jones's Temptation – The Lonely Hearts Series – book 3

https://www.amazon.com/dp/B08775663R

https://www.amazon.co.uk/dp/B08775663R

The Lonely Lord

https://www.amazon.com/dp/B07S1X5NBZ

https://www.amazon.co.uk/dp/B07S1X5NBZ

The Drummond Series:-

Lady Lou the Highwayman – Drummond series Book 1

https://www.amazon.com/dp/B07NDX3HV2

https://www.amazon.co.uk/dp/B07NDX3HV2

Saving Captain Drummond – Drummond Series Book 2

https://www.amazon.com/dp/B07NFBRZFG

https://www.amazon.co.uk/dp/B07NFBRZFG

Lord Livesey's Bluestocking (Amazon Storyteller Finalist 2018)

https://www.amazon.com/dp/B07D3T6L93

https://www.amazon.co.uk/dp/B07D3T6L93

Return to the Regency – A Regency Time-travel novel

https://www.amazon.com/dp/B078C87HVX

https://www.amazon.co.uk/dp/B078C87HVX

My Foundlings:-

The Foundling Duke – The Foundlings Book 1

https://www.amazon.com/dp/B071KTT9CD

https://www.amazon.co.uk/dp/B071KTT9CD

The Foundling Lady – The Foundlings Book 2

https://www.amazon.com/dp/B072L2D7PF

https://www.amazon.co.uk/dp/B072L2D7PF

Book bundle – **The Foundlings**

https://www.amazon.com/dp/B07Q6YLND4

https://www.amazon.co.uk/dp/B07Q6YLND4

Mr Bailey's Lady

https://www.amazon.com/dp/B01NACMFVJ

https://www.amazon.co.uk/dp/B01NACMFVJ

The Spy Series:-

My Lord the Spy

https://www.amazon.com/dp/B01F11ZRM8

https://www.amazon.co.uk/dp/B01F11ZRM8

My Earl the Spy

https://www.amazon.com/dp/B01F12NG8E

https://www.amazon.co.uk/dp/B01F12NG8E

Book bundle – **The Spying Lords**

https://www.amazon.com/dp/B07RV3JQFP

https://www.amazon.co.uk/dp/B07RV3JQFP

The Captain's Wallflower

https://www.amazon.com/dp/B018PDBGLK

https://www.amazon.co.uk/dp/B018PDBGLK

The Four Sisters' Series:-

Rosalind – Book 1

https://www.amazon.com/dp/B00WWTXSA6

https://www.amazon.co.uk/dp/B00WWTXSA6

Annabelle – Book 2

https://www.amazon.com/dp/B00WWTXRWA

https://www.amazon.co.uk/dp/B00WWTXRWA

Grace – Book 3

https://www.amazon.com/dp/B00WWUBEWO

https://www.amazon.co.uk/dp/B00WWUBEWO

Eleanor – Book 4

https://www.amazon.com/dp/B00WWUBF1E

https://www.amazon.co.uk/dp/B00WWUBF1E

Book Bundle – **The Four Sisters**

https://www.amazon.com/dp/B01416W0C4

https://www.amazon.co.uk/dp/B01416W0C4

The Inconvenient Trilogy:-

The Inconvenient Ward – Book 1

https://www.amazon.com/dp/B00KCJUJFA

https://www.amazon.co.uk/dp/B00KCJUJFA

The Inconvenient Wife – Book 2

https://www.amazon.com/dp/B00KCJVQU2

https://www.amazon.co.uk/dp/B00KCJVQU2

The Inconvenient Companion – Book 3

https://www.amazon.com/dp/B00KCK87T4

https://www.amazon.co.uk/dp/B00KCK87T4

Book bundle – **An Inconvenient Trilogy**

https://www.amazon.com/dp/B00PHQIZ18

https://www.amazon.co.uk/dp/B00PHQIZ18

The Complicated Earl

https://www.amazon.com/dp/B00BCN90DC

https://www.amazon.co.uk/dp/B00BCN90DC

The Unwilling Earl (Novella)

https://www.amazon.com/dp/B00BCNE2HG

https://www.amazon.co.uk/dp/B00BCNE2HG

Other Eras

A Very Modern Lord

Years Apart

About the Proofreader

Joan Kelley fell in love with words at about 8 months of age and has been using them and correcting them ever since. She's had a 20-year career in U.S. Army public affairs spent mostly writing: speeches for Army generals, safety publications and videos, and has had one awesome book published, *Every Day a New Adventure: Caregivers Look at Alzheimer's Disease*, a really riveting and compelling look at five patients, including her own mother. It is available through Publishamerica.com. She also edits books because she loves correcting other people's use of language. What's to say? She's good at it. She lives in a small town near Atlanta, Georgia, in the American South with one long-haired cat to whom she is allergic and her grandson to whom she is not. If you need her, you may reach her at oh1kelley@gmail.com.

Printed in Great Britain
by Amazon